Out of Time: a Time Travel Novel

Cliff Ball

Published by Cliff Ball Books, 2022.

Prologue

They had to escape from this period. The people they were visiting in the 1600's thought they were witches and the spawn of the devil. Historians had warned the schoolteacher about visiting Salem, Massachusetts, during the Salem Witch Trials, especially with a dozen twelve-year-olds in her care. The teacher had Doctor John Hawking and Captain Erickson with the class, but the villagers were chasing after them, and there was no way to get to the shuttle without significantly changing history. Through the Interactive History program, Mrs. Hanson only wanted to show her class what made these Puritans so paranoid, and what happens to people when they were accused of witchcraft. Well, they got more than they bargained for.

Hawking was loudly complaining, "This is stupid. We should have had a military backup when we go to these time periods. With all the threats to us from the Puritans and the Native Americans, neither of which tolerate strangers on their lands, we're in constant danger. I'm going to file a protest with the President, and insist we get some military backing,"

"What about interfering with time by bringing advanced weapons, armor, and everything involved with a military operation?" asked Erickson.

"We have the technology to make our weapons appear to be muskets, so why not? We can then have the soldiers wear whatever uniforms from whatever time we're in, and that will solve that!" insisted Hawking.

"Well, let's worry about that when we get back."

After leading the witch-hunters through the forest for over an hour, the time travelers managed to finally lose them. The school kids thought this was cool, while their teacher was frantic. Erickson led them all back to the holographically disguised shuttle, which was disguised to look like a small house. Once they were back inside, and everyone was accounted for, Erickson piloted the shuttle back to the *USS Einstein*, which was waiting in orbit. On the ship, Mrs. Hanson and her class went to the room that was a temporary classroom, while Hawking and Erickson went to the bridge. On the bridge, Erickson was asked by Yeager, "How did it go, Captain?"

"It didn't go well. One of the villagers got it into her head that we were more than just strangers, so we were accused of witchcraft. Mrs. Hanson tried to argue that we weren't witches, which made them even angrier, especially since it was a woman who was arguing with them. So, within minutes we had the whole angry-mob-with-fire-and-pitchforks coming after us. After our little disappearance, we might as well be witches to them. Remind me never to let any historian or schoolteachers convince us to let them travel to Salem of the 1690's. Now, we can return home and see what other adventures we have in-store for us."

The *USS Einstein* traveled forward to 2157. Once back in their own time, the sixth graders would be doing their e-book reports on what happened in the Salem Witch Trials of 1692. After Hawking and the others had returned from the first missions through time, the government decided there would be a no-interference policy for the past, a sort of Grandfather Paradox Policy. The idea was, through the previous experience, that if anyone interfered in anything significant to the timeline, that when you returned to your period, you may not exist because your ancestors may not have survived a certain period in the time you tried to fix. Hawking said this was all theory and he didn't know if the person would disappear from history if they returned to the present, but he didn't want to find out.

Contaminating the timeline without meaning to could be a real possibility with the Interactive History program the Department of Education had thought up recently. Too many American children knew far too little about their history, so with the use of a time traveling starship, they could learn from first-hand experience. Hawking disagreed with this, but convinced Congress to pass a Grandfather Paradox Act, making sure nobody would interfere in the natural flow of history. Sure, Hawking was becoming rich and famous because of this because school districts, historians, and others paid him to take them back in time, but he still cared about not contaminating the timeline.

Hawking was also worried about when those rogue time travelers from the beginning of his first trips through time were supposed to interfere with the original missions, but he had no idea when in the future they were from. Another worry was the fact that the *Time Tripper* had been built without his knowledge; he wondered what other things had he done that the government had turned around and gone behind his back to do one their own? He would never know. Now, government contracts were going to the lowest bidder for the next generation of time traveling starship.

These new ships and with Commander Robinsons' help, could go faster than the speed of light if they needed to use the suns' gravity to jump through time, which didn't happen very often, since they almost always found fluid time access points. Robinson had also experimented with using black holes to travel through time, which wasn't quite working out the way he thought the experiments would. All the black hole experiment did was make the ship stay stuck in the event horizon, going nowhere, making it nearly impossible for the ship to leave or be rescued, so now Robinson would have to invent a whole new way to get the ship unstuck from a black holes' event horizon.

Hawking made sure he held the patents to his time device, which required the new stardrives to work; he wanted no one, but mostly the government, to go behind his back and build another timeship without his knowledge. President Williamson assured the scientist that anything having to do with the secrets of time travel was now solely Hawking's responsibility; there were no longer secret government labs or secret time traveling missions. Doctor Hawking still wanted to know what kind of missions had occurred previous to Hawking going on his first official missions, but all Williamson would say is that it was classified higher than the security clearance that Doctor Hawking had been given by the powers-that-be.

Hawking had been asked by some Smithsonian Institute historians if he could take them to observe moments like the Boston Massacre, the signing of the Constitution, the War of 1812 and the British burning the White House, the various battles of the Civil War, and other significant happenings in American history. They wanted to record everything for posterity so the Smithsonian Museum could accurately portray everything instead of guessing on a few moments in history.

He was a bit overwhelmed with all the requests for his time and the attention he was receiving, so he finally hired a secretary and an agent so that he wouldn't have to deal with everything so directly. How he ended up as the go-to-guy for trips through time, he wasn't sure - all he wanted to do originally was to figure out how to time travel. Since he enjoyed history, it really didn't bother him all that much to go back in time and show everyone how history had happened. What bothered him was, what would happen if someone messed up the timeline like he and the others did the first time they went through time, would they be able to fix it again? So, he started reflecting on how he went through this whole time travel scheme the first time.

Chapter 1

"Computer simulations are complete. The theories on time travel could become scientific fact once we find a suitable spaceship to complete the experiment. Has anyone located the suitable ship we need for time travel?"

"Yes, sir, Doctor Hawking. NASA engineers have searched every shipyard and have found a ship like what you were looking for. At the moment, it's a derelict ship about to be mothballed by the current owners. They buy old military ships and use the parts off those ships for colony and passenger ships. They're asking for quite a bit of money before they'll even consider selling the ship to us. Would that be a problem?" asked the NASA official.

"No that is not a problem. I have quite a few investors, so money is of no concern to me. I'll inform them of the ship in question, and then I shall go out to look at the ship before I make a decision. Now, what's next?"

The year was 2156, and the scientist was Doctor John Hawking, a brilliant astrophysicist, quantum mechanics theorist, and was considered the ultimate expert on time travel. The United States government and its science community had long ago abandoned the banning of cloning, so the unborn Doctor was an almost complete genetic copy of one Professor Stephen Hawking, who was one of the greatest scientific minds of the late twentieth to early twenty-first centuries. The only thing changed to the genetic makeup was the ALS that Stephen Hawking had been afflicted with. As the clone of Hawking was maturing inside of his mother, scientists were uploading into the clones' unborn brain, various facts and theories so a great scientist could be born. John Hawking was born in the year 2121, in Silicon Valley, California, to Raymond and Allison Hawking, who were descendants of that branch of the Hawking family. At the age of four months, the clone exhibited his brilliance by forming a complete, coherent sentence in less than a week after voicing his first word. At two years old, John was writing and coming up with his own theories, along with mathematical equations nobody had ever seen before, on his rather low-tech family computer. When he was ten, he graduated from the Massachusetts Institute of Technology with a Bachelor of Science in Physics, and then went to Cal Tech, graduating from there at the age of twelve with a Master's in Quantum Mechanics.

However, John became somewhat rebellious at fourteen and decided he didn't want to what everyone wanted him to do, so he decided to become a real teenager and act like one. His parents were thrilled with the idea, but his rebelliousness irritated government scientists who were counting on him to deliver the greatest idea in human history. John was introduced to drag racing by his father; he found that he enjoyed it, and so he began racing vintage cars from the early twentieth to mid twenty-first century, becoming a regular fixture at dragstrips across the country. Car owners in NHRA, NASCAR, and Formula One watched the future scientist, since he was a brilliant racer, and offered him chances to drive their various vehicles, but John declined knowing what his future held for him.

On one fateful, clear summer day, he was gearing up for a race in a 2007 Chevrolet Corvette Z06 against a major rival driving a 2010 Ferrari. John had tweaked the 454 cubic inch engine he had installed so he could get as much power out of it as possible. The two racers made their way into their respective cars, waited for the green light to go, and when they were given the green light, both cars shot off like bullets. Near halfway, John was going over two hundred miles an hour, when his Corvette shuddered and began to flip over. Fortunately for John, his car was equipped with the most advanced safety equipment currently available. However, when his car stopped flipping over four hundred yards from where it began to flip, it looked as though he hadn't survived the crash. The car itself appeared as if it had been sent to the crusher in a junkyard. John woke up three days later in the hospital intensive care unit and learned the extent of his injuries. His left leg had multiple breaks; a hip had multiple fractures, a broken collarbone, fractured sternum, five broken ribs, a broken arm, and a concussion.

While healing from his multitude of injuries, he began watching numerous old science fiction movies and television shows, mostly because he had always been fascinated by the accuracy of new technologies some of those shows seemed to have predicted. What particularly intrigued him was time travel, especially the various methods used by the shows. The best ideas dealt with spacecraft sling-shotting around a star or black hole. The worst idea, even if it was an entertaining movie series, was the use of a car and some nuclear fuel to travel through time, which didn't seem too practical to his way of thinking. Another none too bright idea was the use of a quantum machine, where a person stood inside and leaped through time letting the space-time continuum take them wherever and not having any control over a destination. Knowing that no scientist in quite some time had worked on time travel theories or had even built anything, John knew he would have to start from scratch.

Young Mr. Hawking started his quest by researching anything and everything written on the space-time continuum by Albert Einstein, Stephen Hawking, and other scientists who worked on quantum theory, wormholes, or anything involving the space-time continuum. Einstein's Theory of Relativity was a good foundation to start from as was Stephen Hawking's mathematical equations of quantum mechanics. John thought that time itself wouldn't slow down the faster an object went at light speed, he theorized normal time would flow at the same rate as it had always done. So, in effect, if a person left Earth on the month of February and traveled for four months at the speed of light or faster, that same person would arrive back on Earth in the month of June the same year. However, add the gravitational effects of either a star or black hole and someone could quite possibly travel back and forth through time, which could add time to your trip if you end up back in your original timeline. Stay in the past for a month, and when you return to the future, an hour would be added, at least in theory.

John also worked on a theory about time being fluid, rather than linear. The theory was that time flowed around us, including the past and future, so the past and future were happening at the same time as the present, just in different dimensions. Figuring out how to access those dimensions was going to be difficult, predicted the young scientist, but he was up to the challenge.

John presented his theories and complete science paper to the science community at the age of twenty-six, ten years after his unfortunate drag racing wreck. Taking only an hour to present his theory and how it could be achieved, John also took the time to answer questions from his colleagues. For the most part, the scientists were skeptical, but the biggest interest in the time travel theories came from the United States government and NASA. Mainstream scientists thought the whole idea of time travel was foolish and not worthy of their attention. NASA, after more than a century of working on superstring theories, speed of light travel, and whether black holes and wormholes could send a person to the past, was more than ready to help John Hawking. The United States government was interested because of the historical research they could do, at least that's what they told Doctor Hawking.

Eight years of conducting simulations on supercomputers and refining the matter-antimatter fuel the colonies in deep space used, all that was lacking was a spaceship. The device invented by Hawking for time travel was the size of a four-cylinder engine. Its job was to communicate to the ships' computer where in time the ship was and when to shut down the engines. If the device worked wouldn't be known until it was used for the first time. Over the years, Hawking had even managed to persuade businesses to become investors for the project. He had Microsoft supply the software, IBM the computers, and various other high-tech companies he could use to buy the spaceship once it was found. After his final computer simulation was complete and the NASA engineer had told Hawking about the found ship, Hawking arranged for his private shuttlecraft to take him to the coordinates of the ship graveyard.

The history of the ship, as told to Hawking, had a rather violent past. Commissioned in 2129, the *USS George Patton* was built as a dreadnought Star Destroyer class warship. China had declared war over a planet in Alpha Centauri, even though the United States had colonized the planet two years before. China wasn't remotely interested in Alpha Three until mass quantities of minerals not found on Earth were discovered and then China decided to have some interest in the planet. The war began when a squadron of fighters attacked and destroyed an American frigate ship on its way to Alpha Three, and then proceeded to attack an orbital weapons platform being built in orbit above Alpha Three. The colonists, who had some foresight about needing to defend the colony, had purchased one pulse cannon from the military, and then activated it and destroyed six of the ten ships attacking the platform. China then tried to attack installations in the Sol System, trying to cripple the American space program. Before the war, technologies such as a complete shield grid for ships and subspace communications weren't considered important. Communications between Earth and a starship two light years away would take four hours both ways and sometimes the messages were badly degraded by the time the communication was received. Shields consisted only of deflectors for debris and at times weren't very effective. Ships returned to Earth pockmarked and even seriously damaged by space debris.

As Hawking's shuttle approached the shipyards, which orbited the Mars moon of Phobos, he read how the *Patton* had ended up in the graveyard. In a battle close the Alpha Centauri System, the *Patton* destroyed or disabled six Chinese Dreadnought Super Carriers before a fighter from one of those carriers sent two missiles into an exhaust manifold of the *Patton*. Once the missiles exploded, life support was destroyed, along with communications, there was no control over the weapons, the engines became damaged, and created a major hull breach that couldn't be contained. The captain put the *Patton* on automatic pilot in the direction of the Sol System before he and the rest of the crew died from asphyxiation. Fourteen months later, the *Patton* arrived near Jupiter as a ghost ship and was towed back to Earth, where the crew was buried, and the ship towed to Mars and forgotten by the powers that be.

As the shuttle made a pass around the *Patton*, Hawking saw the breaches in the hull - burn marks where fires had raged and a large hole where the missiles had exploded inside the warship. The *Patton* was a technological marvel for the time, advanced technology that worked quite well for seventeen years and had yet to be improved on. The design of the ship was a combination of an Earth bound Second World War battleship and a second-generation NASA space shuttle, making it a tough, yet agile warship. Hawking docked the shuttle at the *Patton's* docking port and then boarded the *Patton* so he could personally inspect the interior. While he was docking, NASA contacted him and told Hawking that an engineer would be joining him on the *Patton*.

The NASA engineer and Hawking boarded the *Patton* at the same time, they shook hands, and Hawking said, "I'm Doctor John Hawking, and you are?"

"It's an honor to finally meet you, Doctor Hawking. I'm Lieutenant Dennis Robinson, United State Air Force, attached to NASA to help you out. Now that we're on board the *Patton*, as far as I can tell from what little I've seen so far, it'll take at least six months to overhaul this ship. So, where should we begin?"

As Hawking turned on his flashlight since the ship had no power, he responded with, "Would the backup power generators function now after all these years, and where would they be?"

"I'm not sure the backups would power up now, but we'll find that out in a few minutes. Engineering is where the generator's located, two decks below us. Let's get going."

The two men located an access hatch a few minutes later, which would lead directly to Engineering. Ten minutes later, they stepped onto the Engineering deck, and they began to look for the generator. As they searched, both men passed near the huge hull breach, and if it wasn't for the gravity boots they wore, both men could have stumbled and floated out of the ship and into space.

The engine room was in a horrible mess. The fusion engine was beyond repair, and one of the exhaust manifolds had ripped through the deck, destroying all the life support systems. This had apparently caused a massive fire, resulting in a lot of damage, but since the hull had been punctured, the fire didn't spread further. Support beams and fiber optic cables were hanging dangerously, the beams looked ready to fall loose and cause even more damage. Robinson found the generator, booted up the computer with his handheld device, which brought the ships' power online, albeit a bit slowly, grid by grid. After making sure nothing would short circuit. Robinson and Hawking decided to make their way to the bridge, five decks up and ten sections forward.

As they entered the bridge, both men came to the realization that nobody had been here in nearly fifteen years. Robinson went over to a computer station and logged on. There was an artificial intelligence program, but after all these years, the engineer thought the AI may have corrupted. However, it didn't matter since an upgrade would be installed once Hawking made his decision. After touring the bridge, Hawking said, "Lieutenant, I have made my decision, this is the ship I want. I will take care of the arrangements and I assume the government has you overhauling this ship, so I'll trust you with the new engines and the installation of my time device. Please contact our shuttles and we can begin a new era in human history."

The *USS George Patton* was bought by Hawking's investors and towed to the *Luna Shipyards*, which orbited Earth's moon and in geosynchronous orbit over the Tranquility Sea United States Air Force Base. A small contingent of Air Force and Army engineers were assigned to overhaul the *Patton* and install everything Hawking wanted installed. Since this project was classified, security was considered top priority, so Homeland Security assigned more personnel to the *Luna Shipyards* to make sure nothing was leaked to the media, until such a time when the public would be informed of the project.

As Hawking worked on his program to launch the ship back through time, he also worked with the creator of the newest version of the artificial intelligence matrix to make sure the AI accepted the possibility of time travel. Unlike the previous version that was installed in the *Patton*, this matrix would be friendlier and would take orders like it was programmed to do. After all, according to Isaac Asimov's Laws of Robotics, robots and the like were to obey humans no matter what. Hawking had no desire for the AI to overcome its programming to overthrow their human masters and make humanity slaves or have all of them killed off. Finally, six months later, the ship was ready for its first real world test in time travel and the new name for the ship would be announced at an upcoming press conference.

The date was September 10, 2156, when Doctor John Hawking announced his breakthrough to Earth, Mars, and all points outward that contained human civilization. There was a select group in person for the conference at the *Luna Shipyards*, while the general public was either watching on television or on the internet, waiting for the rumored momentous announcement this scientist was going to make. The media had taken to calling Hawking a crackpot, so much so that the general public was skeptical of the initial claims of time travel but were interested in seeing if Hawking would fail in a spectacular fashion.

When Hawking was finally ready, he began by saying, "Ladies and gentlemen, in person and those watching from around the colonized galaxy, welcome to this press conference on the topic of my scientific breakthrough.

"Many of you have been wondering, for what probably seems like a long time, what I've been doing, and there are some who may even know what this is about. Well, the United States government and NASA have helped me realize my dream by helping me make my theories on time travel a reality in the here and now. As of three days ago, we have a working starship capable of time travel. The first real world test will begin after this conference. First off though, let me explain how I came to make a theory into reality.

"When I was a teenager, I was involved in a serious car wreck, which landed me in the hospital for many months and no way of leaving my room on my own. In that time, I began to watch a lot of science fiction movies and old television shows that led me into reading the theories of time travel and the space-time continuum. I meticulously researched everything on what I saw in those movies and came upon one that seemed realistically plausible. Some plots dealt with launching though time using a stars' gravitational field or a black hole. The one I was particularly interested in used matter-antimatter for fuel and launched the ships into impossibly faster-than-light speeds. Currently, our ships are powered by fusion, so the top speed hovers at seventy-two million miles an hour. Due to the limits of this technology, there is no way to get any more power than that out of the engines. Matter-antimatter stardrives will be able to reach just above the speed of light, which, with current technology available, is as fast as we can go. Now, I'm open for questions,"

"Doctor Hawking, Mike Louis of CBS News, Mars Bureau. Has this project cost the American taxpayer any money and will humans pilot the ship in its first real test?"

"The American taxpayer has not and will not pay for this. I have numerous investors who have paid for all my research and the ship we're using. If needed and requested, I will provide a list of investors and what they donated within the week. As for the first test, androids will be the test subject as to reduce risk to humans," answered Hawking.

"Doctor Hawking, do you honestly think antimatter is worth the risk to time travel?" asked a scientist over the net.

"Yes, I do. Matter-antimatter has been used as a source of power in our colonies for over fifty years. In the right hands, it is very safe," reassured the Doctor.

"What about the fact that the first ever use of that material blew up half of the moon Io late last century?" asked the same scientist.

"Something like that won't happen, everything is much, much safer now. From my research, that explosion was a result of poor management, not from a particular fault of the matter-antimatter. Like I said, it's very safe in the right hands," Hawking insisted, dismissing concerns his colleague seemed to have with matter-antimatter.

"Doctor, have you named your ship?" asked someone else.

Relieved that someone changed the subject, Hawking answered, "We have. It's named the *USS Albert Einstein*, after the famous early twentieth century scientist who came up with the Theory of Relativity." After a few moments of silence, Hawking asked, "Anyone else have any other questions?"

"I do, Doctor. I'm Professor Jerry Tyler of Cal Tech. You want us to believe you took ideas from two-hundred-year-old science fiction movies on how to travel through time. What do you think we are, children?"

"I do not think any of you are children. I happen to think the people of the twentieth century had wonderful and unique ideas on what they thought the future might be like. Quite a few technological advances came out of watching or reading science fiction, because scientists like us wondered if they could make fiction into science fact.

I think as long as rules are set on time travel, we should have no problems,"

"Are you trying to reassure yourself or us on all of these so-called security measure which are supposedly in place?" asked Louis.

"I never said anything about security measures. What are you talking about?" asked a bewildered Hawking.

"Do you know about Colonel Drayka?" persisted the newsman.

"I've heard of him, why do you want to know?"

"I believe he stole secrets and classified documents from NASA, under the nose of the Department of Homeland Security, and took those to the Japanese Technology First Society. They are a known terrorist group, considered by everyone, including Japan, as too extreme. Since obviously they'll get word about time travel, they could use the same technology themselves, go back in time, and destroy any country Japan has tangled with, either in war or trade. Do you realize what might happen then?" Louis questioned.

"Mr. Louis, this is not as bad as you'd like everyone to think. The JTFS is no real threat as their goals are simply not attainable. They're a bunch of hooligans looking to gain publicity, which it seems, they have. Anyone have any other questions before the test begins?"

"Where is the *Einstein* going in time?" a text-based message from the net asked.

"The ship will travel back to 1969 to witness the first moon landing by Neil Armstrong. The androids will be sure to record everything so we can make sure they went to 1969. From our perspective, they will be gone for approximately ten minutes so we can tell they left to begin with," remarked Hawking.

"Wouldn't the *Apollo* astronauts see the *Einstein*?" asked Louis.

"What a preposterous thing to think. The *Einstein* will orbit Venus and view the historical event from there. Nobody should even see the ship, considering all it will be is an observer of an event in the past."

Hawking glanced at a digital display on the wall that told them time, "Ok, now it is time to launch the ship."

The *USS Albert Einstein* undocked from the *Shipyards* and flew out to open space between Earth and Mars. The ships' computer, with the help of Hawkings' time device, scanned subspace for a wormhole or a tear in time. Ten minutes later, the time device activated the new stardrive when, according to the data that Hawking was receiving, the computer found a tear in time. As the *Einstein* built up the energy to open a ripple in time, the ship became distorted, rainbows of light appeared around it, and the *Einstein* flashed out in a bright, white light. The whole scene was broadcast in real time by a ship that was recording the event from a few million miles away. Seconds later, the *Einstein* was in 1969.

As the *Apollo 11* astronauts began to land on the moon, the *USS Einstein* began orbiting Venus. The radio receiver on the timeship tuned into the old NASA frequency right as Neil Armstrong was beginning to speak his most famous words, "One small step for a man, one giant leap for mankind." The *Einstein* stayed for another hour and promptly left for 2156 to complete its mission.

Meanwhile, on Earth, at Mount Wilson Observatory in California, an astronomer had been scanning the various planets in the solar system when he noticed a large object orbiting Venus. With his powerful telescope, the astronomer zoomed in on what appeared to be a spaceship of some sort. He took pictures of the ship until it departed, and then he went to develop those same pictures. When the pictures developed, what he saw troubled him, so he called NASA. NASA informed him that he should show up at Edwards Air Force Base in two days with the photos and to not be tardy.

Two days later, the astronomer, Carl Sagan, arrived with the pictures at Edwards. A military policeman escorted Sagan to the base briefing room, where he saw five men, one of which was the Governor of California, Ronald Reagan. Two of the others were dressed like

Marines and the other two were men in black suits. One of the Marines, who had the rank of Lieutenant Colonel, came over to Sagan and introduced himself, "Mr. Sagan, thank you for coming. I'm John Glenn and we are here to see what you have in those photographs,"

"I'm honored to meet you, Lieutenant Colonel. These photos are of a spaceship orbiting Venus at the same time as the moon landing. For the hour or so it orbited Venus, I closely observed it and took these pictures. When I developed these, I realized NASA should be informed and here I am,"

"What were your findings, Mr. Sagan?" asked Reagan.

"I found the name of the ship, whose flag it seems to travel under, what appeared to be a NASA symbol, and quite possibly the year this ship is from," remarked Sagan.

"Could you be a bit more specific?" asked one of the men in black.

"Who, may I ask, are you?" demanded Sagan.

"Who we are is of no importance to you if you cooperate and ask the right questions. Now, go on and answer the question, Mr. Sagan."

Must be the FBI, Sagan thought to himself. Then he said out loud, "Very well. The name of the ship is the *USS Albert Einstein*, flown under the flag of the United States. A number, 2156 AD, was present, so I assume that's the year it came from,"

"You're kidding!" blurted the other Marine.

"No, I'm certainly not. Look for yourselves." Sagan then handed the photos to Glenn. "What do you think?"

"I'd say it's better than having something the Soviet Union built being out there." Glenn understated.

"Were the *Apollo 11* astronauts threatened in any way?" asked Reagan.

"I don't think so. A ship bearing the name of Albert Einstein, appearing to observe the first moon landing, must be for historical research or something to that effect. Einstein and his Theory of Relativity dealt with the space-time continuum, so maybe a scientist in the future finally figured it out and conducted their first time travel test. Mind you, I'm just guessing." remarked Sagan.

"President Nixon wants all of this to be considered classified and never to be talked about. Mr. Sagan, we will need these pictures of yours and we will be watching you in the future. Thank you for your cooperation gentlemen and good day." remarked the talkative man in black as they both walked out of the briefing room.

One hundred and eighty-seven years later, the *Einstein* approached the *Luna Shipyards*. The media decided to leave once the ship successfully returned from the past, since there was no spectacular failure and there would be no opportunity to destroy Hawking's life's work with wall-to-wall coverage of the failure. As the time ship docked, an Air Force airman approached Hawking with a rusty box and said, "Mr. Hawking, I was told to bring this to you."

"What is it?" asked the scientist.

"That would be none of my business, sir. All I was told was to deliver this to you and leave. Here you are, sir." the airman left after he handed Hawking the box.

Hawking looked at the box and saw at the top where it had *"USS Einstein, 2156"* written there. Hawking undid the latch, opened the box, found a manila envelope with a typewritten note, all dated July 23, 1969. Hawking read the note and then looked at the people who were involved in his project with an odd look.

"What's wrong, Doctor?" asked Congressman Miller, who supported Hawking in Congress.

"According to this note, an astronomer based at Mount Wilson Observatory saw our ship orbiting Venus. He took pictures, told NASA, the governor of California, John Glenn, and two federal agents. The pictures are in this envelope,"

"You were right about the *Apollo* astronauts not seeing the *Einstein*, but I guess you didn't figure on someone watching the other planets at the same time. Who saw our ship anyway?" asked Charlie O'Brien, computer programmer for the *Einstein*.

"According to this note, Carl Sagan saw the *Einstein*. I would say we now know how he came up with all those interesting ideas on the future. These pictures show the *Einstein* in clear detail, including the name, flag, and year. What we need is a way to disguise the ship from being seen, maybe some sort of holographic imaging system. Now that the ship has docked, we'll download and review all of the data gathered from the trip through time." stated Hawking.

Chapter 2

A week later, Doctor Hawking and Congressman Miller were called to the White House for a meeting with President Williamson. The President got straight to the point by saying, "Congratulations on a timeship that works, Doctor,"

"Thank you, sir. Unfortunately, the ship was seen in 1969," Hawking said.

"I know about it because Congressman Miller here sent me his report. After reading the report, I went through documents classified by Nixon until this week, and I found out what his orders were. He wrote the letter you received, Doctor, and ordered the pictures to be locked up until this year. He also ordered Sagan, Governor Reagan, and Glenn not to reveal what little they knew. Nixon himself kept quiet for the rest of his life," briefed the President.

"You didn't ask me here to tell me that did you?" asked Hawking, impatiently crossing his arms.

"Of course I didn't. I called you here because I want the *Einstein* used for a lot more time traveling," the President stated, in a rather condescending tone.

"That is why I invented time travel, Mr. President," Hawking said, thinking he was stating the obvious.

"I realize that Doctor, but I mean I want your ship to intervene in problems NASA, our country, and some of our interests have had over the centuries," stated Williamson.

"I don't know what your advisors told you but changing history so cavalierly would disrupt the flow of the space-time continuum to such a degree that we would never know if the Earth we knew existed until we returned to this period. After all, I'm an independent scientist, not a government scientist,"

"If it weren't for the federal government, you wouldn't be the person you are today, Mr. Hawking. All those corporate sponsors didn't just help you out of the goodness of their hearts – we the government pushed them into it. In effect, you owe us, Doctor," Williamson stated, matter-of-factly.

"You…. you're blackmailing me?" asked a dumbfounded Hawking.

"No, I'm just telling you where your priorities should be. Let me put it to you this way, if you don't cooperate, we will accuse you of treasonous acts against the United States by using time travel to subvert the government. You do know what the Homeland Security Department does with traitors. So, are you doing to be more cooperative?"

"Yes, sir," Hawking imagined being locked away in one of those horrible DHS camps. It made him depressed.

"Now, we have done numerous what-if scenarios on many events in United States and world history and have narrowed down what we think are the least troublesome to the space-time continuum. I had a list made up of what you and the new crew are going to do and what you aren't going to do." the President handed Hawking and Miller a printout. "Want to discuss this?

The time traveling items to do:

Try to help at the Alamo.

Stop Wounded Knee Massacre.

Re-route a ship near the *Titanic* to rescue more people.

Help Anne Frank and family survive Concentration Camps.

Stop President Kennedy's assassination.

Fix *Apollo 13*, *Skylab*, and *Challenger*.

"Half of these are major events, the *Titanic*, Anne Frank, and Kennedy for example. With the *Titanic*, why not just keep the ship from sinking instead of re-routing another ship?" asked Hawking.

"According to the scenarios we've done, the *Titanic* not sinking would do more harm than good. As a result of the sinking, shipping lines were moved further south, safety on board ships was considered more important, and communications between ships became regulated. In one scenario, the *Titanic* sinks anyway, in the place of the *Lusitania*,"

"Certainly makes sense to me. What's your take on Anne Frank?" asked Miller, before Hawking could reply, as the scientist was about to argue with that kind of reasoning.

"We figure that if Anne and Margot Frank are inoculated against typhus, both will survive instead of dying less than a month before Bergen-Belsen was liberated. Beyond being liberated we don't know what'll happen to Anne and Margot. Maybe Anne will be a famous writer or Margot the head of the Red Cross or something similar in nature," remarked Williamson.

"If we save Anne Frank, why can't we stop the Holocaust altogether?" asked Hawking.

"We investigated that, and no matter what we do, the Holocaust will occur, either in the 1940's or a different decade. Kill Adolf Hitler in World War One, and Heinrich Himmler could begin a different kind of NAZI party, one that could be far worse since Himmler was the Gestapo Chief. If someone were to kill Himmler, someone else might create some kind of NAZI Germany with a Holocaust of some form or another. Stopping World War One has too many variables to even try to stop, so World War Two was going to happen anyway. So, all you'll be doing is to make sure Anne and Margot survive World War Two,"

"If we inoculate Anne from getting typhus, then why would the Germans send her and Margot to Bergen-Belsen?" asked Hawking.

"No matter what we do, the Germans would send them there anyway. Now let's move on to our next topic. Did you have a problem with JFK being assassinated?" asked Williamson.

"Yes. Do you realize that if Kennedy was kept from being assassinated, it could cause major disruptions in the space-time continuum? You could ruin NASA, every President after him could be different, and the Soviet Union could become even stronger. You name it, it could happen," argued Hawking.

"I respect your opinion, Doctor, but it's just that, your opinion. In ours, we believe that if Kennedy wasn't killed, NASA would have bigger growth, we'd have a moon base long before 2025 and a Mars colony before 2040. We would have left the solar system before 2045 and would be further along in our space exploration by now. We also think the only change in presidential succession would be Lyndon Johnson would never get the chance to be the president. Added to that, we also think Robert Kennedy and Martin Luther King, Jr. would not be assassinated and live much longer lives. Any other problems, Doctor?"

"Yes, I do have a couple more problems. First off, why isn't the *Columbia* on the list to fix, while the *Challenger* is on the list? Secondly, why do you want whoever the new crew is and I to help the Alamo?"

"We thought we could add the *Columbia*, but when we did the research first and then realized we couldn't, the decision was made not to add the shuttle to the list. Because of the *Columbia* disintegrating upon re-entry, NASA grounded the three remaining shuttles and soon came to realize that they needed to produce a safer, more advanced, and less breakdown prone spacecraft. I suppose if anyone on the *Einstein* wants to try to keep the *Columbia* safe, go right ahead. I personally think it's just not the wisest thing to do. As for the Alamo, thousands of Mexican soldiers against less than three hundred volunteers just isn't fair. Also, before you complain about Wounded Knee, that was revenge by the Seventh Cavalry to avenge the defeat and death of General George Custer at Little Bighorn. We want you to help the Sioux defeat the rest of that Unit," explained Williamson.

"I suppose all of this makes sense to you, but all I wanted to do was observe events in history, not be a part of those events," complained the scientist.

"I believe the *Einstein* was part of the events during the first moon landing, thus changing history, even though the government squashed that information until recently. I'm not going to discuss how much every President since the 1940's have written about a certain time traveling starship, but I can say it could make a good novel or a movie. Do you have anything else to complain about, Doctor?"

Hawking was speechless after hearing President Williamson say the *Einstein* has already been involved in American history, making Hawking wonder if his being alive was some big conspiracy by the United States government. Realizing the ship had already gone in time and changed everything, Hawking wondered why he still remembered John Kennedy's assassination and both space shuttles being destroyed, so he asked, "Since the government knows about this and assuming everything has already changed, why are we still talking about going back in time and changing everything?"

"That would be the ultimate paradox, which is your area, not mine. Now, here are the don'ts:

American Revolution.

War of 1812.

First Civil War.

Lincoln's assassination.

Little Bighorn.

Spanish-American War.

World Wars one and two.

Korean, Vietnam, and Gulf Wars.

Second Civil War of 2015-2025.

Any questions?" asked Williamson.

"Why can't we prevent Lincoln from being assassinated?" asked Miller.

"Lincoln's death has even more variables than Kennedy's did. We think that as long as Lincoln stayed alive, the South would have been more resistant to the Reconstruction, even though the Radical Republicans made it worse in the original timeline. Under Lincoln, the South may have been under martial law far longer than they were previously. We also think that no president who was born in the South, whether from Arkansas, Georgia, Tennessee, or Texas, would have become the President of the United States if Lincoln hadn't been assassinated. The South also needed to learn for themselves to give their black citizens Civil Rights, instead of being forced to do so by carpetbaggers and the like who swept into the South after the War. Atlanta may have never gotten the 1996 Summer Olympics or become the economic force they are today,"

"Still really doesn't make much sense to me. I do have another question though: why not interfere at the Battle of the Little Bighorn, thus preventing the Wounded Knee massacre altogether?" asked Hawking.

"The soldiers at Wounded Knee were fourteen years removed from Little Bighorn and nary a one of them were with Benteen and the others who had separated from Custer. Wounded Knee was revenge, pure and simple, and that is why it needs to be stopped. We considered going to Gettysburg during the Civil War and getting Custer killed in action, thus preventing the whole altercation. Unfortunately, there are too many variables in that situation. Any other questions related to your mission?" the President inquired.

"No, sir, I have no more questions for the missions themselves. I do, however, want to know who the crew of the *Einstein* will be?"

"The Joint Chiefs of Staff has finished their search for qualified personnel, and most of them were deployed on deep space missions, but they will begin to arrive within the week, then you can start the mission. I can, however, confirm the identity of the captain of the starship; it's Captain Janet Erickson,"

"Is she the same Janet Erickson who set the fastest speed and time from Earth to New Titan in Alpha Centauri round trip a few years back?" asked Miller.

"Yes, that's her. She wondered if she could make the trip to Alpha Centauri in less than two years at maximum speed with not stopping, so she decided to modify a shuttlecraft with the most powerful engines available. The round trip took twenty-one months, five days, three hours, and ten minutes. Once she arrived back here, she was given permission to spend the next six months on leave to recover. After her leave, Erickson rejoined the crew of the *USS Sally Ride* as its new captain, after having been the first officer, and she has been there for the last five years," explained Williamson.

"Would she happen to know what her new assignment is?" asked Hawking.

"She does, as a matter of fact. The Joint Chiefs weren't even considering her until she saw your press conference a few days after you had held it. She said she loves a challenge, so she contacted the Pentagon to ask about becoming the captain of the timeship. Erickson was given command on the spot without second thought from Command. I believe the second-in-command will be Kevin Smith, who's in charge of operations on the *USS Neil Armstrong*. We already have the engineer, Lieutenant Robinson, since he already knows how the ship functions. Our pilot will be Wes Yeager, an experienced combat pilot, who happens to be a direct descendent of Chuck Yeager, the first to break the sound barrier. We will also have a small contingent of soldiers in case you need them, but they will be in stasis when you do require their services,"

"Aren't you forgetting to assign a doctor to the *Einstein*?" asked Miller.

"We didn't forget. We feel that if the crew is in constant danger, they can always return to this period to get some help if someone is injured. Unfortunately, we don't have the technology for a holographic doctor like the one on of your favorite television shows, Doctor Hawking. Is there anything else we need to discuss?" asked Williamson.

Hawking and Miller looked at each other and shrugged, so Williamson ended the meeting and told them the next meeting would occur once the everyone assigned to the *Einstein* had returned to Earth.

Chapter 3

Fifty years further into the future, time travel had become a regular event, so much so that nobody paid any attention to it any longer. There were, however, people who wanted the timeline back to the way it was before Doctor John Hawking interfered by building that time machine of his back in 2156. Nobody knew why, but certain events in the past were remembered two different ways, both the original version and the altered version, and there was no valid scientific theory that could explain it despite many attempts to do so. There were two-dozen people gathered who were part of the FBI, NASA, and some actual historians whose jobs it was to go back in time. They met to figure out a way to stop Hawking so that the space-time continuum could be restored back to its original state.

"I've read all non-classified documents on Doctor Hawking's first time travel missions. Some of these don't quite add up since those missions are still classified because Hawking is still alive. I, however, have files from some of us who went to the past, and I think I know where to begin," remarked the leader.

"If some of us have traveled to the past to fix this already, then where is our time ship and how come none of us remember any of it?" asked one of the rogue FBI agents.

"You don't remember any of it, because we haven't done it yet. I have missions for each and every one of you. I know when, where, and how we will get our ship. I personally will travel to 1924 to begin operations to stop Doctor Hawking,"

"What's in 1924, boss?" asked one of the NASA time travelers.

"It is the year J. Edgar Hoover becomes the Director of the Federal Bureau of Investigation. I will go back to take over his position, since according to these files, Hoover was from the future, and these files appear to be written by me. The real J. Edgar Hoover will disappear on May 9, 1924, thanks to me. All I need is some surgery to look like him."

"What do the rest of us get to do?" asked the same NASA time traveler.

The man who was soon to become J. Edgar Hoover explained to everyone present what he or she would each be doing in the past. Hoover didn't bother to tell them that Hawking and his people were resourceful, especially since he knew one of the time travelers personally.

A few days later, after Hoover received surgery to look like the original Hoover, he and a few of his people infiltrated the *Luna Shipyards* to steal the most advanced timeship currently in existence. The docks had been expanded over the years, mainly to accommodate the *USS Albert Einstein*, which had been turned into a museum. Everything on the first timeship had been deactivated, so there was no chance that the rogue time travelers could steal the *Einstein*. The ship the infiltration team wanted was a quarter the size of the *Einstein*, had a more efficient stardrive, and was equipped with weapons. The ship itself had curved wings and a hull extending outwards, giving it the look of a steel bald eagle. The infiltration team successfully boarded the *Timeship (TS) Max Planck* while the power for the *Shipyards* was cut, leaving the station dark and having no way to detect a ship leaving the docks. The *Planck* was powered up, its transponder was deactivated, and the stolen ship flown to a small base in the asteroid belt.

When everyone who was going to the past boarded the ship, they activated the device to search for access to fluid time, found what they were looking for, and went through the hole in space-time. The *Planck* entered the twentieth century, headed for Washington, DC, where the ship landed softly on top of the Department of Justice building in 1924, and the soon-to-be FBI Director drifted inside with his own agents. Once everyone who was supposed to be in 1924 was safely inside, the *Planck* few off with other missions its rogue time travelers needed to do. The original J. Edgar Hoover was sitting at his desk when his doppelganger barged in, and pointed a sinister looking weapon at the twentieth century human.

"Who are you and what do you want?" demanded the original.

"Don't you recognize me? I'm you and I'm here to take over your job."

"You expect me to believe that? Get out of my office before I have you thrown out!"

The doppelgangers' answer to the original was to aim his weapon and fire. The energy from the weapon first melted off the skin, then the muscle, and then the skeleton was reduced to dust. The future Hoover used a weapon that made sure the victim was in complete pain until they succumbed to death. The new Hoover had his agents clean up the mess, and he soon got to work. In the 1930's, after Hoover caught gangster Al Capone, he used more of his knowledge of the future to rob Capone's vault in Chicago. The vault had millions of dollars in it, along with quite a few liquor barrels used during the Prohibition Era stored there too. In the 1980's, reporter Geraldo Rivera thought Al Capone's vault had never been opened and might still have some treasures housed inside. So, on television, Geraldo opened the vault, and much to his embarrassment, nothing was in the vault but cobwebs and dust. Hoover also used his knowledge of the future to blackmail various Congressmen and Presidents so that he could stay in power. Hoover also sent one of his agents on a mission to 2145 to set up the Japanese Technology First Society, just so they could recruit Joseph Drayka.

Back in 2156, on a man-made island twenty-five miles southwest of the main Japanese islands, Colonel Drayka had some news for the leader of the JTFS, so he walked into the leaders' office, and said, "Good morning, sir, I have news,"

"What would that be, Mr. Drayka?"

"The United States has conducted its first time travel test," stated Drayka.

"What's your point?"

"You would like to dominate Earth with Japanese technology, correct?"

"That is our primary goal. What has time travel got to do with it?" asked the leader, trying to manipulate Drayka into doing what Hoover wanted.

"Do you not see? If we were to take control of the Americans' time machine, we could go anywhere in the past to have Japan control the world by the time we returned to this time period,"

"Do you have any idea where this time machines located?" asked the leader.

"I can find out since the American media reported the time travel test and more than likely also reported the time machines' location. The media can never keep anything a secret, so I'll access the Net to find out."

"You had better get to it before the Americans begin using time travel full time."

Drayka turned on his palm-sized device and logged onto the Net. He browsed news sites until he found what he was looking for, copied the information, and then printed it out. There were eight pages, mainly background on a Doctor John Hawking, who had invented the means to time travel. Drayka, after thoroughly reading the documents, said, "In order to use this time machine, it has to be hooked up to both a stardrive, which uses matter-antimatter as fuel, and the computer. This new stardrive has the capabilities to launch the ship past the light speed barrier,"

"Since when has anyone been able to achieve light speed?"

"There is nothing here that says when light speed was broken, but this article does say that the first real world test was a certified success. The timeship is docked at the *Luna Orbiting Shipyards*, which, I know is very lightly defended by a couple gun turrets and one or two fighter ships. The name of the ship is the *USS Albert Einstein*," stated Drayka.

"Ah, named for a great scientist, very good indeed. Where in time do you propose to go once you hijack the *Einstein*?"

"I suggest we go back to World War Two, where I believe most of Japan's problems began. We go back to December 7, 1941, and assist the Imperial Fleet in not only attacking Pearl Harbor, but landing on Hawaii, and then help them go on to attack the United States mainland. After this, we will drop an atomic bomb on Washington, D.C., and then do the same to London, Moscow, and what's left of Berlin. I think doing that'll make Japan the Supreme World Power on Earth. We return to this period to bask in the fortune we've found ourselves in,"

"Mr. Drayka, you've really put some thought into that scheme. Would you inform Fleet Admiral Yamamoto of your plans?"

"No, I will not share in the glory of those who failed to begin with. I will do this all myself." Remarked Drayka.

"I wish you good luck then. Tell our fighter pilots to ready their fighters for an attack on the *Shipyards*."

At sunset, fifty short-range star fighters, SF-15E Super Novas, which were based off American fighter-craft, launched towards the moon. Due to inordinate amounts of technology devoted to the latest in stealth technology, the fighters were equipped with the same kind of radar absorbing material the F-117 used to use, essentially making the fighters invisible to current radar sensor systems. Ten minutes later, the *Shipyards* came into view, so the strike force split into groups and attacked. Colonel Drayka and his group attacked the docks. Five freighters, a tug, and the *Einstein* were moored there, so Drayka ordered all ships but the *Einstein* to be destroyed. Since there was no one on board the six other ships, Drayka had no problems destroying those ships. As they finished off the ships, Drayka and his infiltration team docked next to the *Einstein* to board the deserted timeship.

When Drayka finally made it to the bridge, he contacted the other members of the strike force, "Red Banzai, this is Team Leader. We have taken the prize. What is your status?"

"Have successfully destroyed the command center and escape pods are on their way to the *Freedom Space Station*. We are breaking off and returning home. Good luck. Red Banzai out."

Drayka's team consisted of the pilot, computer specialist, engineer, and the commander for running the *Einstein*. As overseer for the entire mission, Drayka ordered the Chinese computer specialist, "Ming, access the computer so we can be on our way,"

"Yes, sir. Computer, activate all programs related to time travel,"

"Access denied. Only high-level pass codes are accepted to access those files,"

"You're most likely the newest in artificial intelligence, so either tell me now or I'll be forced to hack you, which I can't bear to do." stated Ming.

"Unless you are the American crew, Doctor Hawking, or Charlie O'Brien my programmer, there is a zero percent chance I will tell you willingly. I must also inform you that if you deactivate me, the stardrive and the time machine will not work. I suggest you leave now before the *Luna Shipyards* security finds you here." stated the *Einstein*, matter-of-factly.

"Mr. Ming, ignore this overly chatty computer and override the darn thing." ordered Drayka.

Ming nodded, then took out his hand-held device, and hacked into the *Einstein*. Ming finally gained control of the computer after twenty minutes, and turned over the command functions to Drayka. After running systems check, Captain Yamata asked Drayka, "So, where in time do we go?"

"We will be going to 1941, before the attack on Pearl Harbor."

"Excellent. Lieutenant Yamagu, please set coordinates and Ming, make sure the computer does what we want. Engineer Nagama, activate stardrive so we can be on our way." ordered the captain.

The *Einstein* left the battered *Shipyards* and headed for a place to open up fluid time. The computer had been programmed for this event after Charlie O'Brien had installed the computer into the ship. The new program was a Trojan horse and didn't activate until the right events were initiated. Someone wearing a dark suit, the AI remembered, installed the program. Even though the monitor read December 7, 1941, as the destination, in actuality, the ship was programmed to arrive six years later in a completely different part of the world. The *Einstein* flashed out of 2156 in a rainbow of colors.

The crew awoke from their sensory overload to find that the *Einstein* was approaching Earth. Captain Yamata tried to access the computer and found that he couldn't gain any access to it. Yamagu had been trying to pilot the ship, but she also found that the *Einstein* was not responding to commands. Yamata, who was getting extremely irritated, asked, "Ming, what in the blue blazes is going on with this ship?"

"I couldn't even begin to tell you. The computer won't let me access it, and has locked out any kind of communication with my computer. However, I can tell you when and where we are,"

"Are you saying that we aren't in 1941?" asked an incredulous Drayka.

All Ming could do was nod his head yes.

"Ok, then, when are we?" asked Yamata.

"On the monitor, this says we're in 1947. Our destination appears to be Roswell, New Mexico." Ming stated.

"Roswell? What in the world is in Roswell?" Drayka demanded.

"I think I could tell you," answered Yamagu.

"Out with it Yamagu!" ordered Yamata.

"I don't know if any of you have heard of the UFO that supposedly crashed outside of Roswell in 1947, because up until this moment it had always been a source of mystery. Now, I think we caused the Roswell Incident of 1947,"

"This must mean this whole entire operation was known to the United States government. We've been tricked!" roared a very angry Colonel Drayka.

"How would the United States know we'd hijack their timeship and then send us to Roswell in 1947? Now explain that." asked a calm Yamata.

The engineer, who had come up from engineering since she had nothing to do, said, "I think this is a paradox,"

"A what?" asked a bewildered Drayka.

"A paradox is when something like this happens. We've already been to Roswell, causing the whole alien-United States government conspiracy theories that have grown through time. Somebody in the United States decided to have this whole entire event happen, thus, when he hijacked the *Einstein*, we set up a series of events that led us here."

"Whoever set us up, must've known time travelers would end up at Roswell, causing two-hundred-years' worth of events culminating with those same time travelers, in the form of us, hijacking the ship and ending up in 1947. What I want to know is, just how many secret black ops does the United States have?" asked Yamata.

Everyone, including Drayka, shrugged their shoulders and all of them felt used by some unknown force from over two hundred years in the future. The *USS Albert Einstein* entered Earth and headed for Roswell, New Mexico. Five minutes later, the ship landed on the outskirts of the Roswell Army Air Base. Almost immediately, two-dozen Sherman tanks, a dozen heavy cannons, and over one hundred soldiers surrounded the ship. A General's Jeep pulled up, which prompted the *Einstein* computer to open a hatch in the bridge floor, dropping a rope ladder to the ground. The General yelled up to the crew to come out of the ship, which they did, and they were immediately put under arrest. As they were led off, it put into motion certain events that would culminate two hundred years in the future and lead back to 1947, which created a continuous time loop in this instance.

Two days later, Colonel Drayka was sitting alone in an office in Washington, D.C. His crewmates had been sent off somewhere, making Drayka think they were in prison by now. The United States military flew him to Washington for reasons completely unknown to him. Drayka had known his backers wanted him to go back to 1941 to help Japan invade the United States, but the fact that he ended up in 1947 worried him greatly. Drayka was also supposed to have met up with an agent from his future, which didn't happen since he wasn't currently in 1941, and now Drayka was thinking he was in serious trouble for failing his objective.

After sitting alone for twenty minutes, three men entered the office. One sat down behind the desk, looked at Drayka silently for a minute, and then said, "Colonel Joseph Drayka, formerly of the United States Air Force, currently a member of the organization known as the Japanese Technology First Society. Hijacked the *USS Albert Einstein* to go on a mission to 1941 to help Japan invade the United States, instead you arrived in 1947. What do you have to say for yourself, Mr. Drayka?"

"All I can say, is I think I was setup. I have question for you though: how do you know so much about me?"

"Yes, you were setup. We had no intention of sending you to 1941, so we planted in the ships' computer a series of events that would lead to the landing of a ship at Roswell Army Air Base this year. We know a lot about you because some of my agents in the FBI have been following you for years, which include the so-called leader of the JTFS. We have a great interest in you, Mr. Drayka,"

"*Who are you?*" asked a puzzled Drayka.

Chuckling, the man said, "J. Edgar Hoover, of course,"

Drayka sat in his chair, stunned for a few seconds, then managed to stammer out a few words, "How is that possible? How do you know so much about the future?"

"I know so much, because I am from the future,"

"If what you're saying is true, Director Hoover, why do you need me?" asked the confused Drayka.

"We need you because you can help me and my men reverse engineer the *Einstein* to put it to good use in this time frame,"

"Why can't you just reverse engineer the ship yourselves with your own engineers? You must have someone to help you if you managed to travel from whatever time you came from to be here in 1947?" asked Drayka.

"We are rogue time travelers who are neither scientists nor engineers, and I haven't seen our time ship in years. I will not tell you anything else about where I came from. In the meantime, we persuaded President Truman to have scientists of this time try to figure out the technology. They'll be assembled at Hangar 18 in Roswell at the end of this week. Next week, you and one of my agents will go to Roswell to find out about their progress." ordered Hoover.

Hoover and Drayka began discussing various events in future history and whether they should change time the way they wanted it to be. However, Hoover knew almost exactly when and where the *USS Albert Einstein* would end up, and if possible, Hoovers' own agents would be there to try to stop it.

Chapter 4

Walking into the Oval Office, Hawking said, "Mr. President, we have a huge problem,"

"I know. The *Luna Shipyards* crew escaped as the base was attacked and the *Einstein* hijacked. I would like to know what you think happened to the timeship?" asked the President.

"I think I have a good idea where the ship went. I've done some more research and found that Stephen Hawking thought the United States government had been conducting time travel experiments in the 1990's. The science community thought that was an eccentric idea, but I believe he was right. President Williamson, is this yet another conspiracy which involves me?"

"Yes and no. I assume you've heard of the Roswell Incident of 1947?"

"Of course I have. To this day, people talk about Roswell and what supposedly happened there. There are some who even think aliens from outer space, which we've never come across, were involved. Other than some nutcases, you must know the real answer, Mr. President," remarked Hawking.

"Again, I would have to say yes and no. I may be the most powerful man on Earth, but I don't know everything that goes on around here. I can assure you that I'm being manipulated about as much as you are. Until the *Einstein* was hijacked, I thought my becoming the President of the United States was on my own merit. I've since learned otherwise. Since 1947, a very secret government agency decided to track the *Einstein* through time. This agency knew about me, apparently, and knew about you, totally and completely. I've learned I was supposed to be president because of what happens in 1947. I also now know what we should do to retrieve the *Einstein*,"

"Since this is probably one of those really deep covert operations, I'm willing to guess there's a backup time travel ship somewhere in this solar system all fired up and ready to go," guessed Hawking.

"There is another ship, amazingly enough. Good deductive reasoning Doctor. It's docked at the *Freedom Space Station,* and has been used for some black ops into the past a couple of times. Now that the *Einstein* has been hijacked, they informed me of their ongoing project, and they'll let us use their timeship to retrieve the *Einstein*,"

"So, I've been spied on, in regard to time travel, this entire time?" asked a bewildered, somewhat angry Hawking.

"I assume that would be the case. Why we need covert time travel when you're doing it publicly makes no sense to me. I've been told by the same people who are lending their ship to us, that all we have to do is land at the Roswell base to retrieve the *Einstein*. First off, that's an insane idea. The United States and the Soviet Union were always at a state of alert back then, being in the Cold War and all, and having another ship show up and land uninvited on a military base would invite more trouble than it would be worth. I get the impression we're supposed to fail. What do you think, Doctor?"

"My question is, why 1947? I'm thinking this group wants my technology, or future technology, to fight the Soviet Union. More than likely, it was to get ahead of them technologically. Since they want us to land on a military base, you must have come up with an alternate plan, I would think,"

"I have, since I'm not the complete moron they think I am. I've ordered a shuttlecraft to be assigned to the ship, along with an Army Jeep and military uniforms of the era, which will be stored in the cargo bay. You're also going to need someone to get past the guards, and that same person will have to pilot the second ship back to this time," stated Williamson.

"Who would that be?"

"Me,"

"I have to object, sir. I can't let the President of the United States go gallivanting through time, especially since time travel is still in the experimental stages."

"Sorry, it's already been decided. The Vice President will be in control until we return. We get the *Einstein*, I return with the newer ship, and you go on with your missions. I know how to pilot a starship and all you have to do is program the ship for the return trip. If you're done arguing with me, then meet me on the *Freedom* tomorrow morning, where we will meet the new crew."

The next morning, President Williamson arrived on the *Freedom*, was greeted by Hawking, and they went directly to the docks. As Hawking walked by the windows facing space dock, he saw *TS Time Tripper* emblazoned on the side of this new timeship. This ship was smaller, but had the look of a former warship. Hawking wondered why the ship had such a bland name, but whoever named the ship probably wasn't near his intelligence level, so he blew it off.

Soon, Hawking and Williamson were on board the ship and headed for the bridge to meet the crew. As the new crew was making pre-flight preparations, Hawking and Williamson walked onto the bridge, which Captain Erickson saw, so she said, "President Williamson on the bridge!"

Everyone stood up from the respective posts to salute their Commander in Chief, causing Williamson to order, "At ease. By now, all of you must have introduced yourselves to each other, so I'd like to introduce you to John Hawking, the inventor of the device that will throw us back in time. First off, Dr. Hawking, this is Captain Erickson,"

As each person approached the other to shake hands, Hawking noticed how attractive Erickson was. She had blue eyes, chestnut brown hair, about five feet seven in height, and had an air of confidence about her that he had rarely seen in most women he knew, since most of the women he knew were scientists who didn't care about their looks. She was about five years older than him, which didn't matter to him,

since he had an instant crush on her, mostly because he never had time
to meet women outside of work, and probably wouldn't know what to
do if he had.

On the other hand, Erickson saw in Hawking a typical scientist
- unkempt, uncombed hair, and looking a bit like he needed a good
rest. Not really the kind of man she could write home to her parents
about, not that she was exactly worried about getting married, she
was too committed to her career, and Hawking didn't exactly make an
impression on her. They shook hands, Erickson went back to her duties,
and Hawking met pilot Wes Yeager.

Yeager looked almost exactly like photographs he had seen of test
pilot Chuck Yeager. The thought crossed Hawking's mind to ask the
pilot if he had been cloned too, but decided against it, since it might
be a rude thing to ask. Overall, Yeager seemed liked a pleasant enough
person to the scientist. The next person after Yeager that Hawking
met was Commander Kevin Smith, a fellow who seemed to Hawking
like he wasn't exactly thrilled to be on the *Einstein*, and Smith was
one of those people others wouldn't notice in an empty room. Smith
reluctantly shook the scientists' hand. Lieutenant Robinson, the ships'
engineer was in the engine room preparing for launch, but Hawking
had already met him.

"Is everything and everyone ready to make this trip?" asked
President Williamson once the introductions were over with.

"Yes, Mr. President. If I may be so bold to ask, what are you doing
here?" asked Erickson.

"I will be returning this ship to this time period once we retrieve
the *Einstein* so that all of you can go on the missions that you've been
assigned,"

"I didn't realize you knew how to pilot a starship, sir," remarked
Yeager.

"Once upon a time, I did fly a starship, when I was in the military. I
was in the Top Gun program, where I flew everything the United States

had built between the 1930's and the last war. Mr. Yeager, I suggest you not worry about my capabilities, just make sure you know how to pilot this starship. Are we ready to depart?"

"We are receiving permission from Mission Control, sir. *Freedom* has cleared flight lanes for us to depart, leaving us a clear path to the sun. Robinson has informed me that the version of the device installed for time travel in this ship is only able to launch the ship back in time by using the suns' gravity to activate the device. Apparently, the black ops team installed an early version of Hawkings' invention,"

"I was flirting with the idea of launching a ship back in time by flying around a sun, but thought that was more than a little impractical. I don't know what'll happen, but let's find out, shall we?" remarked Hawking.

Ten minutes passed before they were given the all clear, the ship undocked, and then headed for the sun. On the way, the *Time Tripper* passed ships of various sizes with a variety of jobs that were waiting for the timeship to pass so they could continue with their jobs. The *Time Tripper* began speeding around the sun, the computer activated the machine, and the process of leaping back in time began. A rainbow of light appeared around the ship, the ship became distorted, as if phasing in and out of time. Seconds later, the ship disappeared from 2156 in a blinding white flash of light.

The AI of the *Time Tripper* stopped the ship near Venus since the humans on board were unconscious. As they began to wake up, Hawking queried the computer, "Computer, why did we humans pass out?"

"Standard time displacement; humans were not prepared and blacked out from sensory overload,"

"This must be like the blackouts astronauts and jet pilots experienced when they went through multiple changes in gravity at once. Computer, are we in the designated time frame?" asked Hawking.

"Designated time frame is 1947. Ship is in 1947, so target time has been achieved."

As everyone else woke up, Captain Erickson asked, "What just happened?"

"It was nothing worth worrying over. Going through time causes us to lose consciousness. This is like going through multiple g-forces without pressurized suits in any kind of aircraft. However, we are in 1947," stated Hawking in a dismissive tone.

"Excellent, Major Yeager, set course for Roswell, New Mexico. May I ask, President Williamson, what are we doing in this mission?" asked Erickson.

"We'll have the *Time Tripper* orbit Earth. Some of us will fly in the shuttle to somewhere near Roswell Army Base, and then we'll infiltrate the base. I've had official documents made to get the military to release the *Einstein* to us. In fact, Doctor Hawking and I will be dressed in black suits to make sure we get the ship back under our control. Does anyone have any concerns or questions before we depart?"

"This is what, two weeks after the *Einstein* landed at the base?" asked Commander Smith.

"Yes. What's your point?" asked Hawking.

"Don't you think the scientists of this time period would have figured out your technology, wrote about it, took detailed pictures, and then began to use the technology?"

"I don't think that would or will happen. If it had happened, time travel would have been achieved by the late 1940's, instead of 2156. We wouldn't be sitting here arguing about it if it had happened, so what's your opinion of that, Commander?" asked Hawking.

"How do you know it hasn't happened yet? As far as we know, the Earth in our period might already be changed, much more advanced, and way beyond the first stages of time travel. Or Earth could be completely destroyed because of nations like the Soviet Union being able to get time travel. Have you at all thought about the consequences, especially in centuries where there is no real technology?" persisted Smith.

"Yes, Commander, I have thought about the consequences. As for this century using time travel, no scientist in his right mind would even try to figure out time travel because of the threat from Communist Russia. What is your real problem, Commander?"

"Isn't it obvious, Doctor Hawking? My problem is with time travel,"

"Why, Commander, did you accept this assignment if you have a problem with time travel?" asked Erickson.

"I had no choice. One minute, I was a lieutenant commander in charge of ship operations on the *USS Rick Husband*. The next thing I know, I was promoted to commander and transferred to the *Einstein*. Until I arrived on the *Freedom*, I had no idea I was assigned to a ship that could travel through time. It was three days ago, even though it's now over two hundred years from now,"

"Explain to us why you have a problem with time travel, Mr. Smith." ordered Williamson.

"In my opinion, going around changing history is like playing God. I personally don't want to change what He set into motion,"

"Humans have free will, which God gave to use to figure out what we think is right and what is wrong. I think we should be limited to how far back we could go, don't you think?" asked Erickson.

"How should I know?" shrugged Smith.

"You have a lot of people who agree with you, Commander. You should have seen the message boards, the social media, and blogs light up the day I made my announcement. Some of it was quite unpleasant. However, in my opinion, I think God would prevent us from going any further back than 100 A.D. My reasoning for this is because He wouldn't want us to interfere with the histories of Israel, Egypt, Rome, Babylon, or Greece, all of which have some significance to Judeo-Christian history. If I did want to test that particular theory, I would use this ship, piloted by androids, to go back that far so that no humans would get hurt in case the ship were to get destroyed," explained Hawking.

"Sorry to interrupt, sirs, but we're now orbiting Earth." interrupted Yeager.

"Good. Hawking, Smith, and Robinson will go with me to retrieve the *Einstein*. Erickson, you and Yeager will stay here until I come back with the shuttle, then you two will use the shuttle to board the *Einstein*. Let's get started." ordered Williamson.

The four time travelers went to their quarters to change into 1940's era military uniforms, including putting on all appropriate rank insignias. Williamson and Hawking, however, changed into the black suits that the FBI wore, which included the rogue agents. According to research done by President Williamson on these rogues, they started around the same time Hoover became Director of the Bureau. Their job was to cover up certain technologies that would or could have an impact on American society. Unfortunately, all the files on the rogue FBI agents were classified after 1947, making Williamson wonder if the *Einstein* had a bigger influence on American history than he previously thought. Williamson made a mental note to throw the light on this secret agency once he returned to 2156. In the meantime, he had to report to the shuttle bay.

As everyone was boarding the shuttle, Williamson asked, "Will their radar pick us up even if we're miles away?"

"No, sir. We have stealth capabilities, and the radar of the time is limited. So, we shouldn't have a problem being detected," answered Robinson.

"Famous last words." muttered Smith, who nobody seemed to have heard.

"I assume that the Jeep and the documents we need have been loaded onto the shuttle?" asked Williamson.

"Yes, sir." answered Robinson.

"Commander Smith, please inform Captain Erickson that we're leaving. Set course for Roswell as soon as we're clear of the *Einstein*."

The shuttle bay doors opened, the shuttle flew out, heading for Roswell. Ten minutes later, the shuttle was parked in a remote mountain spot near the base. After the Army Jeep was driven out of the shuttle, the men camouflaged the shuttle, and then drove the thirty miles to the military base. It was a blazing hot summer day as they drove to Roswell Army Base, and unfortunately for the time travelers, the Jeep had no air conditioning.

They arrived at the entrance to the base, and then they waited until the guard gave them permission to go onto the base. The guard informed them that they needed to go to base headquarters to meet the base commander, so Robinson drove the Jeep to headquarters.

"Do you think they might be expecting us?" asked Smith.

"I can't say for certain. Maybe someone who is supposed to be here now isn't, and we showed up just at the right moment. I'm sure we'll soon find out." remarked Hawking.

They arrived at the headquarters and went inside, unsure of what was to come next. They arrived at the General's office, went to the secretary's desk, and Williamson said to him, "We're here to see the General,"

"I'm sorry, but he's busy right now, so you'll have to wait,"

"Ok, thank you." The time travelers sat down in the chairs that were there for such occasions. They ended up waiting forty minutes before the General was able to see them.

After finally being ushered into the office, General Ford greeted them, "Hello gentlemen. I'm going to cut to the chase and assume you're here for the spaceship,"

"Yes, we certainly are. Our agency has sent us to take the ship back to Washington to study it there. We need the ship now, because we have reason to believe someone from the future will come to retrieve their technology before we have the chance to reverse engineer the ship." remarked Williamson, trying to sound convincing.

"Not a problem. I've been ordered by President Truman himself to release the ship to you. By the way, that story your agency gave to use has been a remarkable success," stated Ford.

"What story would that be?" asked a curious Hawking.

"You know, the story about little brown aliens crashing near Roswell, and then the cover story about a downed weather balloon. A stroke of brilliance I must say." Ford looked up at the clock that was hanging on his wall, and then said, "I have to apologize to you gentlemen, I'm rather busy today. Do you people know where Hangar 18 is located?"

"I know where it is, sir." remarked Smith, dressed as an Army colonel.

"All right Colonel, your ship is there. If you can get there yourselves, I'll call ahead to inform the guards that you're coming. If that's all you need, I bid you gentleman a good day." stated Ford, being dismissive.

As the four time travelers made their way outside to the Jeep, Hawking said, "Whoever is behind all of this is sure thorough. We should hurry before the official government agency sends their real agents. I don't know about the rest of you, but I don't want to get caught."

They arrived at Hangar 18, which was painted in desert colors. There was no roof to the structure because the top of the *Einstein* could be seen. Robinson informed the guard who they were, the guard opened a door large enough for the Jeep to drive through, and then they drove inside.

The *Einstein* was lit up by large spotlights, while lots of equipment was scattered beneath the ship on the floor of the hangar, and a ladder was going up into the hatch near one of the landing gears. As the four men got out of the Jeep, an old man with wild white hair walked over to them, and said in a thick German accent, "Greetings gentlemen. I'm the scientist in charge of this operation. I assume you are the people who are here to take this ship back to Washington,"

"Um, uh, yes we are, sir. Are you Professor Einstein?" asked an awed Hawking.

"Yes, young man, I am. What would your interest be in this ship named after me?"

Not sure of what he should say, Doctor Hawking looked over at President Williamson. Williamson's response was to shrug his shoulders. After thinking about what to say, Hawking responded a minute later, "I'm a scientist myself, sir,"

"What kind and what is your field of study?"

"I'm sorry, Professor, but my work is classified at the highest levels, much higher than yours. My work is the kind of classified that could upset the balance of power between the United States and the Soviet Union. I can only say I work in technologies more advanced than the atomic bomb. Please don't inquire further than that, Professor, because I can't say more than that," stated a still over-awed Hawking.

"What could be more advanced in this day and age than the atomic bomb? However, time travel is supposed to be impossible, but here this ship is as proof. My deductive reasoning says none of you are normal military or government agents. I think it's even possible none of you are even from this period of time. Who are you really?" persisted Einstein.

"Mr. Einstein do not push this issue. The United States government wants this top-secret and it will remain that way. Is that understood, Professor?" ordered Williamson.

"I believe I do understand. Take my namesake to do with it what you will. I will not impede you further. Just be careful." with that, Einstein walked away.

"This is what happens when you mess with time travel," groaned Commander Smith.

"Not now, Commander. I'll drive the Jeep back to the shuttle, while the three of you will fly the *Einstein* into orbit. You will then wait for Erickson and Yeager to transfer to the *Einstein*. Let's get going before the actual agents show up." ordered Williamson.

Smith, Hawking, and Robinson boarded the time ship as President Williamson got into the Jeep and left the base. As Williamson was driving out of the base, another vehicle with men in black suits was checking in at the gate. When Williamson was more than a mile from the base, he stepped on the accelerator and sped to the shuttle.

At the same time, the three men inside the *Einstein* had just completed prepping the ship for launch, when they saw on the monitor that two men in black had come into Hangar 18. Professor Einstein began talking to them, which prompted Smith to order Robinson to launch the *Einstein* immediately. As the ship was lifting off, the men in black took out their guns, and began firing at the ship, which did nothing of consequence. The ship shot off for orbit as soon as it was clear of Hangar 18.

"We were so close! Mr. Drayka, you promised Director Hoover the use of that ship. What do you think we should do now?" asked a very angry FBI agent.

"How was I supposed to know they'd be able to retrieve their ship so quickly? Director Hoover seemed convinced I'd be able to help you get the ship. This is not my fault."

"All you have are excuses, nothing but excuses. At least you gave us some technical information; however, since we have no technology from this, your use to Hoover is no longer required. Goodbye, Drayka." Before Drayka could react, the agent shot him in the head, instantly killing him.

In orbit, President Williamson landed the shuttle in the *Time Tripper*. Erickson and Yeager were waiting for him. Williamson asked, "Have you been contacted by the *Einstein* yet?"

"We have, sir. Doctor Hawking would like to talk to you once you get to the bridge. Goodbye and good luck, sir." Erickson and Yeager boarded the shuttle and left for the *Einstein*.

Walking onto the bridge, Williamson ordered the computer to open a communications channel to the *Einstein*. When Doctor Hawking appeared on the monitor, Williamson asked, "Did you need to talk to me?"

"Yes, Mr. President. We almost ran into the actual government agents, who shot at us as we were taking off. Did you have any problems?"

"No problems, but they were entering the base as I was leaving, and it was much too close for comfort. Now you should begin your missions, while I return to 2156 to wait for your return before I return to Earth. Williamson out." The *Time Tripper* headed for the sun and leaped forward to 2156.

Erickson and Yeager arrived on the bridge of the *Einstein*. Erickson then asked, "Are we ready to leave?"

"Yes, Captain. President Williamson has already left for the future, and I guess we're supposed to go about changing history." remarked Smith,

"That is our mission, Commander. Lieutenant Robinson, check the engines before we leave to make sure our twentieth century friends didn't mess anything up. Major Yeager, when you're ready, please conduct a scan for rips in subspace for fluid time, and send us to the past."

When all systems were found to be in working order, Yeager piloted the ship to a set of coordinates where there was a solid point of fluid time to open, and then began the trip through time. Moments later, they were in 1836.

Chapter 5

As the *Einstein* orbited 1836 Earth, the crew discussed and argued over how they were going to help the defenders of the Alamo hold off several thousand Mexican soldiers. Commander Smith complained, "This is pointless. How are the five of us, along with a few soldiers in stasis, supposed to help Davey Crockett and the others defend the Alamo? I think we should just leap forward to our next objective and forget about this one."

"Our next objective is Wounded Knee, 1890. Since this whole incident is a massacre itself, what difference does it make to help the Sioux fifty-four years from now and not the Alamo?" asked Yeager.

"With Wounded Knee, a Ghost Dance was going on at the time the Seventh Cavalry massacred the tribe, all we do is something covert about the Cavalry. With the Alamo, all they have are muskets and they'd never be able to understand our technology since we couldn't help them covertly. I agree with Smith, we forget about the Alamo and move on," remarked Hawking.

"Here's a thought. Why not interfere at Little Bighorn in 1876? From what I understand, the Wounded Knee Massacre happened in revenge for the defeat of the Seventh led by General George Armstrong Custer," stated Erickson.

"I brought up the same argument to President Williamson. He told me that the massacre is fourteen years removed from Little Bighorn and was simple revenge by men who weren't even part of the regiment at the time. The President even told me they tried a simulation in which Custer was killed at the Battle of Gettysburg, but there were too many variables to consider, so that situation wouldn't work. So, are we going to 1890?" asked Hawking.

After finally deciding to leave 1836 Earth, the *Einstein* arrived in 1890. While in orbit, Captain Erickson decided to take the soldiers assigned to the ship out of stasis. When the *Einstein* was hijacked earlier, Hawking thought it was fortunate that the hijackers had no idea the soldiers were there. If Drayka had known, Hawking thought that he might have had the soldiers killed.

Captain Erickson and Doctor Hawking went to the stasis room, entered their security codes, submitted to retinal and handprint scans, and then entered the room when the computer granted them clearance to enter the room. Twenty soldiers had been asleep since three days before the *Einstein* had been hijacked, and had stayed in stasis for two and a half weeks. They were single men, trained in every special-ops unit the United States military had, and knew they would be re-animated when there was a need for them. Captain Erickson walked over to the stasis pod of the commanding officer, entered another set of security codes, the pod opened, and the officer slowly woke up.

Ten minutes later, a fully coherent United States Army major said, "Major Jim Johnson reporting for duty. What are my orders?"

"First off, aren't you even going to ask what the situation is?" asked Hawking.

"No, sir. My orders were to follow orders to the letter once I was reactivated. All I know is that this ship travels through time and the locations of where my soldiers and I are to be of assistance. What is the current situation, Captain?"

"We're in 1890, Major, about to stop the Wounded Knee Massacre. Do you know the background of this situation?"

"Yes, ma'am. Tensions were high due to the Ghost Dance, in which the local Native American tribe thought it would rid themselves of the white men. The Seventh Cavalry decided to deliver upon the Sioux their own brand of justice. Here is what I think we should do: we infiltrate the camp of the regiment and take them out so we can keep the peace. The Sioux, who were supposed to die, won't, and the events in 1972 involving the FBI and the American Indian Movement hopefully will not happen. Are we ready to begin?"

"Yes, Major. All we need to do is wake the rest of your unit and then you can give them these uniforms, weapons, and then meet us in the shuttle bay in thirty minutes. Doctor Hawking and Commander Smith will meet you there." Ordered Erickson.

Thirty minutes later, everyone who was involved in the mission was dressed in the blue uniforms of the 1890's United States Army and they were ready to depart the *Einstein*. All were going dressed according to their rank, except for Hawking, who was given a field commission of lieutenant, while Commander Smith was given the Army rank of colonel. As the shuttle left the bay, Commander Smith asked, "How do we infiltrate them without horses and without anyone seeing or hearing the shuttle?"

"Since its midnight, most everyone should be asleep. Major Yeager will activate the silent running so the shuttle won't be heard, and when we're near the Army tents, he'll drop a ladder so we can begin the operation. We take care of the soldiers, depart, and then let the Sioux do whatever they need to do." responded Major Johnson.

Ten minutes later, the shuttle was hovering over the Army encampment. Before anyone left the shuttle, Major Yeager made sure everything on the ground was quiet. When the area appeared secured, the ladder dropped, everyone departed, and immediately went to work. The soldiers of the future had pistols equipped with silencers, so they stealthily went to every tent and shot every soldier in the Seventh Cavalry. Johnson, Hawking, and Smith located the commanding officers' tent, so they went inside to issue him their orders. They found a very awake Colonel conversing with a very mean looking man in a black suit.

"What in blue blazes is going on here?" demanded the angry Colonel.

"Calm down, Colonel, I know two of these men. Doctor Hawking, how are you?"

Hawking and Smith glanced at each other, with dumbfounded looks on their faces. Hawking finally replied, "Who are you and how do you know me?"

"Who I am is of no importance, but you're a very important person to my bosses, Mr. Hawking. However, I had no idea you would have military strength with you. I was telling the good Colonel here that he was going to have a visitor who would try to wrest his command from him. I was going to advise him on how to prevent a coup d'etat on him. Unfortunately for myself, I didn't count on other variables in this situation."

Before anyone else could speak, Major Johnson took out his pistol, shot the Seventh Cavalry Colonel in the chest, and swung his gun to shoot the rogue agents' legs. The Colonel died instantly, while the agent dropped to the ground. Johnson then said, "My men and I are part of a covert ops team who knows all about the FBI's Black Ops team that you're a part of. If you try anything, I will kill you. Have anything to say?"

"How did anyone know to put soldiers on the *Einstein*?"

"Sorry, that's classified. Commander Smith, could you please search him?"

Smith, who was astonished by the sudden gunning down of the Army Colonel, nervously searched the agent, finding his identification, a locator device of some sort, and what looked like a communicator. Smith handcuffed the agent known as John Magnus. In the meantime, the future soldiers finished up their mission and reported back to Johnson. Everyone boarded the shuttle to head back to the *Einstein*. The time travelers put Magnus into stasis for further questioning once they returned to 2156.

Once Johnson, Hawking, and Smith returned to the bridge, Captain Erickson asked, "What's going on?"

"It appears that we are being followed," Hawking replied.

"So they know where we're going?"

"I'm afraid so, Captain. I think we should be careful when we stop in 1912, however, we do have the upper hand. Agent Magnus didn't seem to know that we had military support in the form of Major Johnson and his men. Hopefully, nobody else will know that either. In some of our missions, I can see where we might have problems with those rogue FBI agents, but we have plenty of leeway on how to enact the missions. Are we still planning to go to 1912?" asked the scientist.

"Yes, Mr. Hawking. Major Yeager, set course for the sun and we will head to 1912 Earth." The *Einstein* left the 1890's.

When morning came to Wounded Knee, South Dakota, Sitting Bull and the other Sioux who hadn't been shot and killed because of the time travelers' interference, went about their day. They noticed the Army encampment was a little too quiet as none of the soldiers seemed to be on patrol or moving about in general. One of the tribal elders went to Sitting Bull and asked, "Do you think we should find out why the Army camp is so quiet?"

"Not right now. I think we should probably wait a day or two before we do that. I don't want the people to get into trouble."

A gust of wind a few days later from the direction of the Army camp had a rotten stench with it, which drifted through the Sioux village. Sitting Bull and a couple of his warriors went to investigate the camp, and found the Army soldiers dead from what appeared to be gunshot wounds. Finding some bullet casings on the ground, Sitting Bull realized the casings were not from current United States Army issued Springfield rifles, and he had no idea how he could find out which kind of weapons the bullets came from. His only thought was to get the tribe to make sure the encampment was erased off of the face of the Earth, and the bodies and equipment were to be burned.

Three weeks later, another Army regiment arrived, and began asking numerous questions about where the Seventh had possibly gone. Sitting Bull had gone back to Buffalo Bill Cody's Wild West Show, so tribal elders told the regiment that the Seventh had left two weeks earlier, headed west. Other than that, the Sioux didn't know anything. Hours later, the Army regiment headed west in the direction the Sioux had said the Seventh went. When they felt they were safe, the Sioux quietly moved north to Canada. Two months later, the Army regiment came back through Wounded Knee, did some searching, and found some bullet casings that Sitting Bull found weeks earlier. They couldn't do anything about it, so they headed back to their fort. The 1972 incident involving the American Indian Movement and the FBI ends up never occurring because no Sioux ended up massacred in 1890.

Chapter 6

As the *Einstein* orbited 1912 Earth, Commander Smith asked, "Why can't we just reposition the *Titanic* so it won't hit the iceberg?"

"Re-routing the *Titanic* would be a bad idea because of the many variables involved. Everything from commercial shipping routes to safety issues at sea are linked to the disaster, so we can't just keep the ship from sinking. Our government investigated keeping the ship from sinking, only to find that in one scenario the *Titanic* sinks anyway, in the place of the *Lusitania* during the First World War," briefed Hawking.

"What are we doing then? Watching everyone die all over again?" asked an incredulous Smith.

"No, we're not going to watch them die. Our mission is to take over a ship called the *Californian* to send it to rescue the passengers of the *Titanic*. The *Californian* was about ten miles from the *Titanic* when it sunk. Nobody on the *Californian* paid any attention to the distress flares or the telegraph signals, so we're going to change that,"

"Why wasn't anyone at their post with the telegraph?" asked Yeager.

"The telegraph operator had gone to bed, so there was no one to take over for the night shift. The captain of the *Californian* didn't move the ship at night because of ice in the water. He did, however, know about the flares shooting off in the distance. Like I said, we get on board and change the situation," remarked Hawking.

"I suppose we are boarding the *Californian* to take it over?" asked Smith.

"As Doctor Hawking said we would do, Commander. My men and I will help secure the ship and its crew, and then we can head to the *Titanic* to rescue as many people as possible." remarked Johnson.

"Engineer Robinson, I read in your files that you know Marconi and Morse Codes. Just how versed are you in these codes?" asked Hawking.

"I know those codes well, sir. I studied communications in college and was briefly assigned to the NASA communications center. However, after being in that career track for a year, I decided to become an engineer instead. You can rely on me to help with the communications between both ocean-going vessels."

Erickson ordered everyone who was going to be on the mission to prepare to depart. Fifteen minutes later, the shuttle was hovering over the *Californian*, which was motionless in the water. The night was crisp and clear as the *Titanic* could be seen in the distance from where the shuttle was hovering. The infiltration team quietly boarded the *Californian* and went into action. Hawking and Robinson boarded the ship seconds later, with Major Johnson, and the three men went to the ships' bridge. The time was 11:15 p.m. when they entered the bridge to find a lone helmsman, who had enough wits about him to ask, "Who are you?"

"Who we are is of no importance to you, but why we're here is important. Where's your captain?" demanded Johnson.

"He's currently asleep in his quarters," responded the crewman.

Johnson spoke into his communicator to order one of his men to go to the quarters of the *Californian's* captain and bring him to the bridge immediately. Three minutes later, two soldiers brought a very sleepy Captain Lord to the bridge. When he saw who was on his ship that wasn't supposed to be on his ship, he angrily asked, "What in the world is going on here?"

"Captain, we're here because something horrible will happen ten miles south of here and we're here to prevent it from happening. To prevent it from occurring, we need use of your ship," responded Hawking.

"On whose authority am I supposed to just up and hand over my vessel to you?"

"On the authority of the United States government, that's who. Are you going to comply without more complaint?"

"You Yanks have no authority over me or my ship, we're in international waters in any case, and I am a subject of His Royal Highness, the King of England. I shan't move this vessel until you tell me what is so bloody important," Lord stated, refusing to turn over control.

"Do you have a pair of binoculars at your disposal?" asked Johnson, who was getting impatient with the Brit.

"Yes. What of them?" asked the irritated Captain Lord.

"Would you be so kind as to go out on deck and look for a ship directly south of us? Then, you will be told as to why we are moving the *Californian*."

Captain Lord took a pair of binoculars out of a cabinet, made his way outside, put the binoculars to his eyes, and scanned the horizon. He saw a faint outline of a ship, which appeared to be going too fast for current conditions. Lord went back to the bridge and said, "My officers informed me earlier that the ship out there is a German liner. What would your opinion be?"

"That ship, sir, is no German liner. It is the White Star Liner, *RMS Titanic*," Hawking informed the captain.

"Ah, yes, the unsinkable wonder of the modern world. So let me get this right: you want me to move my ship because you think something horrible will happen, and that something horrible has to do with the *Titanic*? You people really need to question your sanity,"

"No, you need to question yours. Whatever gave you and the rest of the world the idea that the *Titanic* is unsinkable better think again, otherwise your arrogance can and will cost many lives." replied an angry Hawking.

"I don't care what you say, I still refuse to move this vessel!"

Hawking was getting more than irritated, until the first officer of the *Californian* arrived on the bridge, so Hawking said to him, "Captain Lord here refuses to accept the possibility that the *Titanic* needs help. Earlier today, your Marconi operator radioed the *Titanic* about ice in this part of the ocean, did he not?"

"I believe he did, yes,"

"Did the operator on the *Titanic* respond?"

"As far as I know they didn't. The only reason we're sitting here is because Captain Lord doesn't want to move the ship at night. If you think the *Titanic* needs help, then it is our duty to go and help. The crew of the *Californian* offers its services."

"I'm not changing my mind!" bellowed Captain Lord.

"Captain Lord, it no longer matters what you think, your first officer agrees with us, so we no longer need you. Major Johnson, get one of your men to take Lord to a holding cell, or something similar, and keep him there until this operation is over." ordered Hawking.

As Captain Lord was escorted off the bridge, Robinson rushed onto the bridge. A few minutes earlier, he was in the communications office to monitor the telegraph, and now he reported, "The *Titanic* has sent out an SOS, they relayed their position and stated they're sinking. I responded by telling them we should be there in less than half an hour. The *Carpathia* also responded, saying they'd come as soon as they could." Turning to the helmsman, Robinson said, "Here are the coordinates and please make best possible speed."

"How many people can this ship hold and how many lifeboats are on board?" asked Hawking.

"We can hold nearly a thousand people and we have sixteen lifeboats, but the *Titanic* has more than a thousand passengers. There's no possible way we can't take everyone on board." responded the first officer.

"The *Titanic* has twenty lifeboats, so that's not a problem. We get as many people on board as possible, and then the rest stay in the lifeboats until the *Carpathia* arrives."

As the *Californian* was headed for the *Titanic*, two rogue time travelers were on board the sinking ship, since they thought they were going to stop Hawking from re-routing the *Titanic* to keep it from sinking. They had boarded the *Titanic* with their own purchased tickets at Cherbourg, France, along with other first-class passengers on April 11, 1912. On April 14, the night of the sinking, the two had stayed out on deck for most of the night waiting for a spacecraft of some sort to show up to drop off the time travelers from 2156. No spacecraft seemed to have shown up, and now the *Titanic* was sinking around them. Their planned mission was now out the window, and one asked the other, "Now what do we do? Should we find a way on to the lifeboats or just stay here to die with all the others who don't make it?"

"I think we should try to get to the lifeboats, since a ship is supposed to rescue the passengers. I probably should've read the history of this mission, but I never did and I have no idea when the rescue is supposed to happen. I just know we were supposed to stop Hawking and his people from re-routing the *Titanic*. Obviously, they're not here. So, let's get to finding us a lifeboat to get on,"

"If we manage to survive this total disaster, how do we contact anyone from the future?"

"Well, our leader is going to be in 1924, so we can wait twelve more years and report to him then. We can find out then why Hawking never arrived."

Thirty minutes later, the *Californian* arrived at the location of the *Titanic*. The supposedly unsinkable wonder of the modern world was sinking, while flares were shooting off, lighting up what was a tranquil night sky. As soon as the *Californian* stopped, the *Titanic* lifeboats headed for the new arrival. At first, some of the boats didn't have many people in them, but that changed when the other boats became filled to the brim with passengers. The *Californians'* own lifeboats went out to rescue people, but after an hour, the *Californian* itself was full of rescued survivors. While this was going on, both ships kept communicating until staying on the *Titanic* became impossible.

About an hour later, the aft section of the *Titanic* was standing straight up in the ocean, with almost half of the ship now under water, when a loud, deafening explosion came from deep inside the ship. The ship suddenly broke in two, plunging back into the Atlantic, sinking beneath the cold, icy waters. Of those who had survived, they reported that Thomas Andrews, who was the builder of the *Titanic*, Captain Edward Smith, the men in the engine room, the band that was playing as the ship was sinking, and two hundred and fifty passengers, went down with the ship. Two hours later, the *Carpathia* arrived and took on board those who were left in the lifeboats. Attempts were made to rescue the screaming, freezing people who were drifting in the ocean, but two hundred died from drowning or freezing. Altogether, five hundred and fifty people died instead of the original fifteen hundred who had died in the original timeline.

Two days later, the *Californian* and the *Carpathia* arrived and docked at the New York City docks. The time travelers from 2156 discreetly made their way to the outskirts of the city, boarded the shuttle that was waiting for them, and left for 1940.

The two rogue time travelers managed to get on a lifeboat, board the *Californian*, and remained there until they arrived in New York City, having absolutely no clue that Hawking was on board at the same time. They moved to Washington, D.C. to wait for Hoover to show up. When 1924 rolled around, the two castaways-in-time reported to Hoover. He was fresh from the future, apparently really angry when he said to them, "If the two of you had read any history of the *Titanic* sinking from our time period, you would know that Hawking had diverted a ship to help, instead of re-routing, the *Titanic*. The ship which was diverted was the *Californian*. Weren't both of you on that ship?"

"Yes, we were, but neither of us knew about the *Californian,* nor the fact that it wasn't supposed to be there. I'm sorry that we failed you, sir."

"You didn't fail me. However, I am extremely disappointed in the lack of imagination displayed by both of you. The next assignment is supposed to occur in 1940, so you'll have sixteen years to prepare for the mission. In the meantime, both of you will help me capture Al Capone and his cronies."

In 1912, however, the United States Senate conducted a hearing on the *Titanic* disaster. The time travelers ordered the crew of the *Californian* never to mention their involvement in the rescue of the passengers of the *Titanic*, not to the Senate, not to the newspapers, not to anyone, ever. The official story was that the *Californian* Marconi operator, Cyril Evans, was about to head for bed when the telegraph began clicking with an SOS from the *Titanic*. So Evans woke up Captain Lord, they went out on the deck, and saw the flares in the distance. Captain Lord ordered best possible speed, coming to the *Titanic's* aid thirty minutes later.

After the hearings, changes were made to commercial routes, moving the routes further south to avoid ice. Regulations to communications were written and safety drills were ordered to be a requirement on all vessels. The *Titanic* still stayed in the memories of people and still made into dozens of movies. Eventually, in the far-flung future of the twenty-second century, the true story behind the rescue was made into a movie, becoming a huge box office hit.

Chapter 7

As they were orbiting the Earth of 1940, the crew wondered how they could keep Anne Frank and her family alive through the Second World War. Captain Erickson asked, "Didn't President Williamson tell us what to do or even how to do this?"

"Yes and no. We inoculate Anne, Margot, and their parents from getting typhus while they're still going on with their lives before they go into hiding," responded Hawking.

"The children will probably be in school, and as the only woman on this ship, I think I should try to see about pretending to be a substitute nurse or something so that I can inoculate the two girls. What about their parents?"

"I don't really know. Since this is really a seat-of-our-pants operation, I guess I could just show up at Mr. Frank's business to inform him and his wife of the inoculations, and ask them if they'd like to be inoculated. Other than that, I have no suggestions."

"Did you just say seat-of-our-pants operation? Gee Doc, run out of something scientific to say?" Erickson teased. Hawking crossed his arms and looked unhappy with that remark.

"Good grief, I'm only kidding. I think the two of us should go on ahead with this mission. Major Yeager, please fly us down there and then wait for the order to pick us up. Let's get going, Doctor." Erickson ordered.

The shuttle landed outside the city of Amsterdam, Hawking and Erickson headed into the city, and the shuttle flew off. Even though Germany was occupying the country, the citizens could still come and go as they pleased, but were stopped occasionally by the Germans so they could check their papers. Erickson and Hawking hailed a taxi and once seated inside, asked to be driven to the Hebrew school where the Frank children attended. On the way to the school, some German Panzer tanks rumbled through the streets with German soldiers marching behind. On the corner of one street, what looked like a Gestapo official was ordering two soldiers to put up a picture of Hitler on the wall. The driver of the taxi made a disparaging remark in Dutch under his breath as the taxi drove by the Germans. Twenty minutes later, the taxi arrived at the school.

The two time travelers headed for the nurses' office when they entered the school. When they found the office, they walked inside to find the school nurse talking to a harsh looking woman in a black suit with no indication she was in any sort of military. Hawking whispered to Erickson, "Be careful, this might be someone who is trying to stop us, so try not to do anything out of the ordinary."

"We could always incapacitate her," offered Erickson.

Before Hawking had the chance to reply, the nurse turned to face them, and asked, "Can I help you?"

Erickson replied, "Uh, yes, I think you can. We're looking for Anne and Margot Frank,"

"Those two are awfully popular lately. This nice young lady was looking for them too, so I sent for them. What do you want them for?"

"Their parents asked me to examine them for any diseases they may have." Erickson lied. Then she looked at the woman in black and asked, "What's her purpose?"

"My only purpose here is to make sure your mission fails. I know you intercepted one of our agents back in 1890, so your interference with all of this time traveling stops here!"

The harsh looking woman in black pulled out a very menacing looking weapon that Erickson didn't recognize. Hawking immediately recognized the danger, and without thinking, pushed Erickson aside. He fired his own weapon at the woman, who fell to the floor badly wounded. The school nurse was shocked by this, became angry, and demanded, "What are you doing? This is a school, not a battlefield!"

"Sorry, ma'am, but we're part of a covert American operation, and this woman is a Nazi sympathizer we've been trying to find. However, we still have business with the Frank girls," Hawking quickly stated.

"I suppose that makes sense. What are you going to do with that German scum?"

"Mr. Hawking here will take her back to our base," Erickson nodded to Hawking, who picked up the unconscious woman, and left the school. Erickson continued, "Now, please don't mention this to anyone else. The Germans are everywhere, and we don't want or need trouble."

The nurse nodded her head yes in acknowledgement. The Frank girls came into the office a few minutes later, and Captain Erickson immediately recognized Anne - she had an air of confidence about her and seemed a little on the cocky side. Margot, on the other hand, seemed shy and reserved, because she let her younger sister do all the talking.

"Did you call for us?" asked Anne.

"Yes, Anne. This woman here needs to give you and Margot an examination of some sort. You don't have a problem with that, do you?"

Anne thought about it for a moment, but her curiosity got the best of her, so she asked, "What kind of exam and what is it for?"

"Anne! You know better than to question an adult." Margot scolded.

"Hush sister. I need a reason to blindly do what an adult tells me. Tell me why it's just Margot and I, but nobody else?"

"First off, I'm giving you some shots. Secondly, I can't tell you, Ms. Frank, its classified information. What I can tell you is that the United States is covertly helping people here in Europe, and your family is one of the ones we're helping. Now, can I give you this?" asked Erickson, holding a hypodermic needle.

"Oh, I suppose so." groaned Anne, as she stuck out her arm, and Margot did the same.

Captain Erickson stuck the needle into Anne's arm, and then used a new one when she gave Margot a shot. Anne, in her overly dramatic way, walked out of the office holding her arm like it had been really hurting. Erickson made sure both girls were ok before she left the school, and that the nurse had everything under control. Once Erickson left the school building, she contacted Hawking, who had taken care of the woman in black, and had given the Frank parents their shots with no problems. They called the shuttle, and the two were back on board the *Einstein* a few minutes later.

In orbit, Captain Erickson decided something needed to be done about the interference by the rogue time travelers, "Lieutenant Robinson, is this ship equipped with weapons?"

"Yes, Captain, I made absolutely sure of that. May I ask what for?"

"I think that if we can find the rogue time travelers' ship, and if it's still here, we could destroy it before they have a chance to interfere again. Major Yeager, since there should be nothing in orbit for another seventeen years, would you scan for anything in orbit that isn't supposed to be there?"

Yeager used the ship's sensors to scan Earth's orbit to see if there was another ship in orbit. Since this being 1940, nothing was supposed to be in orbit until the *Sputnik* was launched in 1957 by the Soviet Union. Yeager detected an unusual energy signature in orbit over North America, so he conducted a more detailed scan. The scan showed that it was definitely a spacecraft, much smaller than the *Einstein*, apparently more advanced, but had minimal weapons. Once all the details were interpreted by the computer, Yeager said, "Captain, I found the ship."

"Raise shields and go to red alert. Take us to them, Major, and fire at will when you have a clean shot."

The *Einstein* flew to the other side of Earth, where the other timeship was orbiting. Yeager opened fire, catching the other ship by surprise, while fires quickly appeared when hull breaches appeared since the enemy ship had yet to defend itself by raising its shields.

The rogue timeship did attempt to defend itself by turning around to fire its own weapons at the *Einstein*, but it was too late. The enemy ship blew up after being pounded for twenty minutes, smaller pieces of it became orbital debris, while the larger pieces fell to Earth. On the ground, streaks appeared in the night sky over North America, and everyone assumed they were meteors hitting the atmosphere. A large, unidentifiable chunk of the ship crashed in an uninhabited area of northern Canada, with no one to investigate what crashed into the ground.

"Lieutenant Robinson, damage report," ordered Erickson.

"We have no damage worth noting, Captain. We can time travel with no ill effects from this skirmish."

"Thank you, Major, that's good to hear. Now, make our heading for 1963."

Meanwhile, in the 1940's, word came to the Jewish people that the Germans were taking them captive, the Franks and a few of their friends hid in the attic of Otto Franks' business, helped by a Christian employee. They managed to stay hidden until August 1944, when a tragic mistake cost them their freedom. One of the men had lost his wallet while trying to obtain some food. Another man, who had been suspicious to begin with, reported his find to the Gestapo. The Gestapo immediately stormed the attic and rounded up these rogue Jews. Soon, all of them were in concentration camps.

Anne and Margot ended up sent to the Bergen-Belsen Camp near the city of Celle, Germany in early 1945. The part of the camp they lived in was squalid, people were starving and dying, and lice lived in everything. Anne found out that a friend was living in the slightly better part of the camp, and that friend eventually began giving Anne food. Despite it all, Anne and Margot survived the desolation of the camp through to the end of the war, which was when the American Army liberated the Jews from the camp. A month later, almost the entire Frank family was back in Amsterdam, but their mother had died of starvation at Buchenwald Camp, which was near Weimar, Germany. Unfortunately, Anne also started to become ill around this time. She had a high fever, was coughing badly, and she was delusional. Three months after her liberation, Anne died of viral pneumonia. Margot, on the other hand, lived a full life.

Margot, due to what happened in the concentration camp and her sisters' death, studied to become a nurse. She attended Johns Hopkins University, interned there, and eventually hired on with the International Red Cross. In 1957, she moved to the new nation of Israel to start her own medical practice. During the Six Day War in 1973, Margot assisted the Israeli Army by caring for the wounded soldiers, which was noticed by the government, and the prime minister gave her the highest state honor. Her compassion led her to help the Palestinians to some extent, since she felt everyone deserved to be treated the same.

Years later, in 1995, Margot Frank had become the personal physician of Prime Minister Yitzhak Rabin. On a November day, Rabin was at a rally for peace between Israel and Palestine. Margot was walking in front of the prime minister as they were leaving the rally when a gun went off. Margot collapsed in a heap, while Israeli security immediately took down the shooter, who complained about missing Prime Minister Rabin. Everyone rushed over to Margot, but the bullets intended for Rabin had killed her instantly.

Rabin ordered that Margot was to be given a State Funeral. Heads of State flew in from all corners of the world to attend the funeral. After the funeral, Rabin became more determined than ever to establish a lasting peace between Israel and Palestine. He managed to convince Yasser Arafat to keep his word by providing many incentives for the Palestinian leader, as long as Arafat didn't keep insisting that Israel be wiped off of the map. Many years later, peace was achieved between the two countries.

Chapter 8

As the time travelers were orbiting 1963 Earth, they were once again wondering how they could change an event. Lieutenant Robinson came up with an idea, then said, "Why don't we just phone President Kennedy? President Williamson did give us the number for the Oval Office."

"I hadn't thought of that, thank you, Lieutenant. Major Yeager can you tap into the phone lines to connect us to the Oval Office?" asked Hawking.

"What do you plan on saying to him?" asked Erickson.

"Well, I plan on telling him who we are and that we need to see him. Since 1947, every administration is supposed to have been told about us, so why not?"

"Doctor Hawking, won't contacting the President interfere with some type of Temporal Prime Directive or something?" innocently asked Commander Smith.

"Temporal Prime Directive? Commander, you have been watching or reading too much science fiction. Believe it or not, I do know what I am doing. Major Yeager, have you been connected to the Oval Office yet?"

"Uh, yes, sir. I bypassed the White House switchboard to get the Oval Office directly, and the call is going through now. I'm going to put the call on the bridge speakers."

"This is President Kennedy, who is this?"

"Mr. President, I have a question for you first. Have you heard of the *USS Albert Einstein* and its appearance in 1947?" asked Hawking.

"I don't know who you are, but that's classified. Who is this?"

"This is Doctor John Hawking, Mr. President."

"Oh my.... What do you want with me?"

"We want to warn you about your trip to Dallas, where you'll have an assassination attempt on your life."

"There's supposed to be an assassination attempt on my life? Do you have any proof? Oh, wait, never mind about proof, you're from the future, so of course you have proof. I'll inform my staff that you and whomever else you're bringing with you will be coming here. Anything else you need to tell me?"

"No, sir, nothing else. We will be there within the hour. Goodbye, Mr. President."

"Goodbye, Doctor," Kennedy hung up the phone, called Andrews Air Force Base to see if they could track a beacon with the signature of either the *USS Einstein* or any other ship coming through the atmosphere. Andrews told the president that they would keep him informed.

On board the *Einstein*, Major Johnson said, "I'm going with you. You may never know when you might run into more rogue time travelers and have need of some back-up muscle. I know how to keep a weapon hidden from prying Secret Service eyes. Who else is coming with us?"

"Major Yeager and Commander Smith should go with you so they can look up what happened in the aftermath of Wounded Knee, the *Titanic*, and Anne Frank after we left their respective timelines." ordered Erickson.

"Major Johnson, I think you should bring two of your men with us. Yeager and Smith, report to the shuttle. I will retrieve proof from my quarters for President Kennedy. I should be in the shuttle bay in ten minutes," ordered Hawking.

Once Hawking retrieved his proof of Kennedy's assassination, the men boarded the shuttle and left the *Einstein*. As the shuttle flew through the sky, Hawking activated the holographic imaging system he designed in his spare time so he could disguise the shuttle as a Piper Cub plane. No matter how the shuttle itself looked, the Andrews Control Tower picked up its signal and tracked it to Lafayette Park, across from the White House. The base called Kennedy and acknowledged the time travelers had landed. When the shuttle was on the ground, Hawking disguised it again, this time to look like a locked-up building. He, Johnson, and the other two military men went to the White House, while Smith and Yeager headed for the Library of Congress.

Secret Service agents quickly escorted Hawking and the other three to the Oval Office. President Kennedy stood up from his desk when they came in, shook their hands, invited them to sit down, and then asked the Secret Service to leave the room. Two of them remained, prompting Kennedy to ask, "Didn't I just ask you to leave?"

"With all due respect, sir, we can't obey that order,"

"Why would that be, gentlemen?"

"We feel that these four men need to be stopped from changing history, so the two of us are here to stop them. I respectfully suggest you step aside, sir."

"Contrary to what you might think, I know all about Hoover and his people. My brother, being the Attorney General, has investigated the FBI Black Ops, and found that you people are linked to the future, of which these four are from. I suggest the two of you drop your weapons because if you shoot me or anyone else in this room, ten Secret Service agents and five Marines are ready to bust in here to take you two out. Do I make myself clear?"

The two rogues dropped their weapons as the other agents loyal to Kennedy came into the Oval Office and arrested them. Kennedy calmly went back to his desk, sat down, and said, "Mr. Hawking, I bet you're wondering how I know so much,"

"The thought did cross my mind,"

"I'm not about to tell you everything we know, but I have information dating back to 1947's landing of the *Einstein* at Roswell Army Air Base. There have also been some rumors about a weird occurrence at Wounded Knee in 1890 and the hijacking of an ocean liner right as the *Titanic* was sinking. I'd like to know why you've come back in time to talk to me,"

"As I told you earlier, we came here because your life is in danger and we want to prevent that from happening." responded Hawking.

"Ok then, where is this proof you want to show me?"

"The proof is some film footage we need to show you, which shows you actually being assassinated,"

"This assassination isn't just a threat then, it's for real, isn't it?"

"Yes, it's for real. When you travel to Dallas, you will be mortally wounded by gunfire. Would you like to see the movie footage?"

"Yes, I would, if you don't mind."

A movie projector and screen were set up, and then Hawking ran the film. At first, the official movie of the Kennedy motorcade going through Dallas was shown, and then the Zapruder home movie came on the screen. Kennedy watched the film in horror as he saw himself getting shot in the head, and Mrs. Kennedy trying to get out of the car. Footage of Walter Cronkite announcing the death of the president on live television was also shown. Near the end of the footage Hawking brought, a man was shown being escorted by the police, when he was approached by a man who shot him on live television. The police promptly tackled the shooter.

"I understand everything that went on until that young man was shot down. Who was or is he?" asked Kennedy.

"Officially, according to the Warren Commission, he is your killer. His name is Lee Harvey Oswald; however, most people don't believe he assassinated you," remarked Hawking.

"If nobody thinks this Oswald person actually killed me, then why was he arrested and then murdered?"

"The details are rather murky, even in our own time, we still don't know exactly what happened the day you're supposed to be assassinated. Oswald claimed he was a communist, but the Soviet Union claimed that Oswald was an idiot. Jack Ruby, a member of the

Mob, shot Oswald. We think the Mob, or maybe someone higher up in the government, ordered your assassination. But we just don't know," stated Hawking.

"When I do travel to Dallas, I still want to be in an open car," responded Kennedy.

"You can still be in an open vehicle; we just recommend bullet-proof glass around where you are. We also think you should post your most trustworthy agents inside and around the Dallas Book Depository, along with the length of the route your motorcade is taking. This is all we have to tell you, so we wish you well and hope you lead our nation better than Vice President Johnson ever will. Thank you for your time, sir." After shaking Kennedy's hand, the four men left for the shuttle.

While Hawking and the others were talking to President Kennedy, Major Yeager and Commander Smith were at the Library of Congress trying to investigate what happened after they visited Wounded Knee, the *Titanic* sinking, and the Frank family. According to two references Yeager found about Sitting Bull, he died in 1914, at the age of 80. Sitting Bull had retired from Bill Cody's Wild West Show ten years earlier, and was very popular among the attendees of the shows. The Sioux, who were supposed to be on their reservation where the Wounded Knee massacre would have occurred, had completely disappeared when the Army regiment who were looking for the Seventh Cavalry had come back to Wounded Knee to inform the Sioux they couldn't locate the Seventh. After some investigation, the Army found evidence that the Seventh had been killed, but not by the Sioux. They weren't sure who might have done the deed, but they were sure they had found some advanced ammunition, so they decided to cover up the incident to the public at the time. Twenty years later, some of the Sioux who had disappeared, returned to the States, and told the United States government that they had fled to Canada. The federal government decided to just leave this particular Sioux tribe alone.

References to the *Titanic* were much easier to find. According to the book Commander Smith was reading, the *Titanic* ran into an iceberg two days before they were supposed to arrive in the United States. The ship sent out distress signals, and two ships, the *Californian* and the *Carpathia*, arrived to assist. A few weeks after the disaster, the United States Senate started an investigation and concluded ocean travel needed to be regulated. Communications, ship routes, and safety on board ships were made into international regulations, making everything universal. All passenger ships were required to have on board the recommended number of lifeboats and emergency drills were to be conducted at least once during the voyage. Shipping lanes were moved further south to avoid ice, and communications between ships were to be always required.

"Doesn't look like we changed much of anything as far as the *Titanic* goes," retorted Smith.

"All we did was to make sure more people survived, and we did our job," responded Yeager.

"Whatever. Have you found out anything about Anne Frank?"

"Yes, I have. Unfortunately, she died of viral pneumonia three months after being liberated from Bergen-Belsen. Her diary is still read in classrooms and a movie was still made in the 1950's. Her sister, Margot, did survive, and according to this, is living in Israel with a medical practice of her own. I wonder why Margot is still alive and Anne isn't?"

"I don't know. Maybe God needed Anne to die as a lesson of the horrors of war and the innocent victims who get caught up in war. Maybe Margot is needed for something bigger years from now, and we won't know what that is until we return to our own time."

Before Yeager could respond to Smith's rather morbid observation, his communicator beeped, he answered it, and the two of them were ordered to return to the shuttle. Twenty minutes later, everyone was on board the *Einstein*. Smith described to everyone what he and Yeager had found out at the Library of Congress. Before the time travelers leapt forward to repair the *Apollo 13*, the *Skylab*, and the *Challenger*, Commander Smith said, "I have a question. Since we're fixing all those spacecraft, why aren't we going to repair the *Columbia* shuttle before it starts its re-entry in 2003? We've interfered in everything else after all."

"I did some research before we left 2156, and found that if we attempt to interfere, NASA will keep right on using the shuttles even though every bit of evidence points to the fact that they were too unsafe to keep using. As a result of the *Columbia* breaking up on re-entry, NASA was ordered by the federal government to build the next generation of space vehicles by 2010, with the help of Boeing, Lockheed, and every company that had ever taken an interest in the space program. Richard Branson and Steve Fawcett, two billionaire adventurers, even helped in the funding and design of the new spacecraft, even though they had launched a civilian version and were conducting regular commercial space flights out of New Mexico. Does that answer your question, Mr. Smith?" asked Hawking.

"Yes, it does. Something else is bothering me too. Are we going to September 11, 2001, to stop the attacks on the World Trade Center and the Pentagon?"

"No, we can't do that. The problem with those terrorist attacks began around the end of World War Two, and maybe even further back into the Crusades. Our problems with the Middle East are so dicey, I wouldn't even know where we would start. Do we go back to the early 1800's to assist our Navy and Marines against the Barbary pirates, or do we go further back in time to prevent Islam from ever gaining a foothold in the areas around the Mediterranean? I don't know and I really would prefer to stay out of geo-politics of that magnitude. Commander, can you quit being such a troublemaker for once, because I would like to go on with our mission. Captain Erickson, please go forward with the next mission." Hawking was getting irritated with

Smith's attitude, but he couldn't do anything about it yet. The *Einstein* leapt forward to 1970 to begin the last parts of their mission.

A week after the time travelers visited President Kennedy, he arrived in Dallas for his tour. As the motorcade passed by the grassy knoll and Book Depository, gunshots rang out, and bullets harmlessly slammed into the bulletproof shield the Secret Service had installed for the president. Secret Service agents loyal to President Kennedy responded to the situation quickly. They ran to the grassy knoll and found two men who were about to run. The two men were Secret Service agents who had been with Vice President Lyndon Johnson since he was the Senator from Texas. They said Johnson ordered them to assassinate Kennedy. The plan was for Johnson to be waiting on *Air Force One* so that he could be sworn in as the new President of the United States. Kennedy, upon hearing the news, ordered the immediate arrest of Johnson and whoever conspired with him.

After a thorough investigation by Attorney General Robert Kennedy and the Justice Department, Lyndon B. Johnson, members of the New York Mob, FBI Director J. Edgar Hoover, and some Cuban terrorists linked to Fidel Castro, were all arrested for conspiracy to assassinate the President of the United States. Instead of spending any time in prison, all those involved were immediately executed within a month of the assassination attempt.

With Kennedy surviving the assassination attempt, he used what little knowledge he had of the future to pull the United States out of Vietnam, which resulted in only five hundred deaths of American soldiers, and had no real impact on the outcome of the actual ending - Vietnam became a Communist country. Kennedy made sure NASA would have a bigger backing by the federal government, so that the Soviet Union would never again surpass the United States in space. Kennedy also gave the CIA the go-ahead to get rid of Fidel Castro by any means necessary, so the CIA did what they were told and had all the top leadership in Cuba assassinated and made Cuba a United States territory, with future statehood in mind for it.

In March 1970, Robinson was tasked with the duty to repair the *Apollo 13* and was given all necessary documents to be able to do so. The *Apollo 13* was scheduled for launch on April 11, so the time travelers decided to arrive in March so there would be necessary time to fix the spacecraft. Robinson arrived at Kennedy Space Center after midnight and went to the location where the *Apollo 13* was housed. Robinson located the spacecraft and went to work. He worked on the wires to the oxygen tanks, giving the wiring better insulation, so that they wouldn't overload, which would have caused the tanks to explode like they had in the original timeline. This took Robinson four hours to fix, and no guards, scientists, or other astronauts had impeded his work, much to his surprise. Once he was finished, Robinson made his way back to the shuttle, which amazingly appeared to be a 1969 Ford Mustang, turned off the holographic image, and went inside. The time travelers, once Robinson made it safely back to the *Einstein*, traveled to 1974.

The launch of the *Apollo 13* went smoothly, as did the flight to the moon, and the landing was considered routine. The astronauts, Lovell and Haise, explored the Fra Mauro Highlands of the moon, made two moon walks, and took seismic readings of the area. After being on the moon for twenty-four hours, they were scheduled to leave, so Haise prepped the engines. As the lunar module, *Aquarius*, was achieving thrust to leave the moon's surface, there was a loud explosion in the engine, and the module dropped back to the surface of the moon. Lovell went outside to inspect the spacecraft, discovering that the booster rockets were damaged beyond repair. He called up the Houston Command Center, "Houston, we've had a problem,"

"What's the problem, *Aquarius*?"

"The engines are damaged; we can't lift off the surface. Is there any way we can take off and connect with the command module?"

There was chatter on the radio, and after about five minutes, Houston responded, "That's a negative, *Aquarius*. Once your engines are gone, you have no way to leave. The command module also has no way of landing on the moon. We can get the *Apollo 14* ready to launch and send them to come and rescue you, but that'll take about a week. We've ordered Swigert in the command module to return to Earth. In the meantime, we'll do all we can to get the *Apollo 14* launched. Do you copy, *Aquarius*?"

"Copy that, Houston. We'll turn power down to minimal systems to try to survive for another five days. Please keep us informed Houston. *Aquarius* out."

The *Apollo 14* was sent to the launch pad three days earlier than expected. Swigert had made it back to Earth and was watching the whole thing take place at Space Command. The rocket achieved lift-off, with *Apollo 14* was on its way to the moon, when it exploded thirty seconds later into thousands of pieces, shocking NASA and everyone who watched the rocket being launched. There was no warning that something was wrong and nothing was left of the astronauts or the spacecraft. NASA informed Lovell and Haise of the explosion, who took it in stride.

The two men survived for three more days, but then died from too much carbon dioxide in the lunar module, since the scrubbers weren't designed to be used for more than the trip to and from the moon and the day or so the astronauts were on the moon. President Nixon declared a national month of mourning, and said that if and when a moon base was established, the *Apollo 13* would be considered a gravesite and national monument, never to be touched. Apollo missions to the moon ended like they had in the original timeline, in December 1972.

The *Skylab* was launched into orbit on May 14, 1973, and put into an orbit that was two-hundred and thirty-five miles above the Earth. The *Einstein* appeared in March 1974, after the last official crew in the original timeline had left *Skylab* on February 8, 1974. The mission of the *Einstein* crew was to elevate the space station to a higher altitude, which was scheduled to happen when the shuttles were scheduled to launch in 1979, but the shuttles were launched much too late to save the station in the original timeline. So, the plan was to use the *Einstein* shuttle to tow *Skylab* about three hundred miles further into orbit. Major Yeager piloted the shuttle, used grappling hooks, and pulled the station into an altitude that Hawking thought appropriate. This was so that the space station wouldn't have a degrading orbit and fall to Earth. Once the station was safely put into the right orbit, the *Einstein* leapt forward to 1985.

As *Skylab* was being moved by the *Einstein*, alerts at the Houston Space Command, formerly known as the Lyndon B. Johnson Space Center in the previous timeline, started blaring. Everyone involved with maintaining *Skylab* was trying to figure out what was happening, when they saw the station moving to a higher altitude. This panicked the scientists and the military men in the command center, they thought the Soviets might be starting something. The administrator of NASA was informed of what was happening, who told everyone what was happening to *Skylab* was considered top secret. He told them that he couldn't tell them why the station was moved, only that there must've been a good reason for it being moved, so they shouldn't worry. Once he got back to his office, the administrator called President Nixon to inform him that the time travelers had just appeared and had moved *Skylab*. Nixon appreciated the information, made sure any and all information about the time travelers was officially struck from public record and disavowed. Nixon, doing what previous presidents had done since Truman, recorded this visit and archived it for future generations, but it also had the effect of increasing his paranoia.

In 1985, before the January 28, 1986, lift-off of the *Challenger* space shuttle, Robinson managed to get access to the solid rocket boosters, one of which had its O-Ring seal fail when the *Challenger* lifted off. Robinson replaced the O-Rings so that they wouldn't fail, even with cold temperatures. As Robinson was working, NASA tracked the *Einstein's* orbital trajectory and informed President Reagan, even though they only knew that a shuttle from the ship had landed in Florida, but didn't know if anyone was interfering in the current timeline. Once Robinson was done, he left 1985, with NORAD tracking the transponder from the *Einstein* shuttle, which the time travelers hadn't changed when they were first tracked in 1963 by Andrews Air Force Base. The *Einstein* left orbit and went forward in time, while the government of the 1980's was trying to figure out why the time travelers were there, but nobody ever figured it out. The *Challenger*, with teacher Christa McAuliffe on board, took off and made into Earth orbit. The astronauts themselves completed the mission they were ordered to do, and McAuliffe taught her class from space. The space shuttle also made it safely back to Earth.

Chapter 9

President Williamson was waiting for the *Einstein*, when he saw a bright light appear near the sun. He waited for a few minutes, then contacted the *Einstein*, "*Einstein*, this is *Time Tripper*. Come in *Einstein*,"

"This is the *Einstein*. Good to hear your voice, Mr. President. We've been gone a month from our point of view, how long has it actually been?" asked Erickson.

"Good to hear from you too, Captain. Since I arrived from 1947, I would say that I've waited about an hour for all of you to return. I have yet to contact NASA or Washington, because I thought I'd leave that honor to you, Captain Erickson."

"Thank you, sir, I appreciate the offer. Yeager, open a channel to Houston."

Yeager attempted to establish a communications link to Houston, but was unable to contact anyone. Fifteen minutes later, he informed Erickson that he was unable to make contact with Houston, other communications sites around the globe, or even the government for that matter. Erickson hailed President Williamson, "Mr. President, we can't seem to raise anyone. All we get is silence,"

"That's very odd. Have you tried all frequencies?"

"Yes, every frequency we know of, digital and analog." Then, Yeager interrupted Captain Erickson to tell her something, then she said to Williamson, "Mr. President, apparently, we're receiving a weak signal from Earth. Yeager says it's a distress signal being broadcast in Morse code. Please give us a little time to decode it." Thirty seconds later, "The computer says the distress signal is more of a warning, which has been broadcasting for at least one-hundred and fifty years,"

"What exactly does the message say?" asked Williamson.

"What it says is: 'Attention all ships returning to Earth, stay away, repeat, stay away. Nuclear war devastating planet, suggest all ships return to Mars or wherever they are traveling from, by order of the President of the United States.' The message ends there and then it's repeated, sir,"

"What did you people do?" asked a stunned Williamson.

"I'm sorry, sir, I have no idea. Everything was fine when we left 1985, something could've happened years after we left, which may have nothing to do with us." Hawking replied, at a loss at what to say.

"We're going to find out what went wrong and make the appropriate changes when we do discover how whatever happened, happened. I'll come aboard the *Einstein*, and we can land together in Washington, D.C."

As both ships went into geosynchronous orbit over North America, the devastation on the ground was noticeable. The land looked dead over wide areas, lakes appeared dried up, and the clouds had a menacing looking quality to them. As President Williamson walked onto the bridge of the *Einstein*, he ordered, "Scan for life signs,"

"I knew nothing good would come from time traveling," muttered Commander Smith.

"Commander, did you say something?" asked a visibly irritated President Williamson.

"No, sir."

"Right answer, Commander. Major Yeager, have you completed your scans?"

"Yes, and the scans show that approximately four hundred and twenty-three million humans are alive on the surface, compared to eight billion in the previous timeline. I've found horrifyingly high levels of radiation coming from Los Angeles, Houston, Detroit, Chicago, Cheyenne Mountain in Colorado, and New York City. I also searched the AM/FM bandwidth and found nothing discernable."

"Well done, Yeager. We'll soon find out what all of you did to change the timeline this severely. Yeager, fly this ship down to Washington." Williamson ordered.

As the *Einstein* descended, the nuclear wasteland of Earth was even more disturbing than what it appeared to be from orbit. The Great Lakes area was blackened, as the lakes appeared nearly devoid of water. Chicago and Detroit were no longer there, they were so completely destroyed that it appeared they had never existed at all. Human activity appeared to be almost non-existent. As the ship flew further east, the worse everything appeared. Major battles looked to have been fought in Philadelphia, New York City, Boston, and Washington, D.C. Williamson ordered Yeager to land the *Einstein* outside the Pentagon, or what was left of it, since the Pentagon appeared to be falling in on itself. Yeager mentioned that there appeared to be some minor power fluctuations coming from somewhere inside the military headquarters, quite possibly the basement. Everyone left the *Einstein,* and headed for the Pentagon computer lab, which was in the basement and had a separate power supply. Major Johnson and his men guarded the time travelers as they made their way through the building.

The Pentagon was in a horrible mess. Some of the corridors had collapsed, and one side of the building was completely destroyed. Arriving in the second-floor basement, where they detected the power usage, the time travelers were shocked that the air conditioning was running and everything was devoid of dust. In the computer lab, a lone computer was running with a screensaver. The computer appeared to be an early twenty-first century relic, of the Hewlett-Packard variety. Doctor Hawking walked over to it, sat down in the chair at the desk, and touched the mouse. He looked up the time, date, and when the computer was last used, and then said, "Someone has been using this computer for a few years. Regular entries in the Word program have been made and it appears as if someone has managed to hack into the super-secret classified files of the FBI and CIA,"

"Before you accessed the computer, I would have assumed everyone here would have been thrown back to some type of Dark Ages and wouldn't know how to use computers." remarked Erickson.

"So the question here is: when, why, and how did a nuclear war start?" queried Williamson.

"In order for me to answer that, I'll have to access the archives."

Searching for nuclear war was easy to find, and the reasons for it was just as easy. The seeds of nuclear war began with the Star Wars Defense Program, and ended with the installation of the last satellite in the grid, placed in orbit by the *Challenger* shuttle on January 30, 1986. The Soviet Union thought the United States had been bluffing about the satellite defense network, so the Soviets launched two ICBMs at two American satellites a month after the grid was activated. The satellites' automated defense systems not only destroyed the missiles, but also activated nuclear missiles in silos all over the United States. Nuclear missiles rained down on Kiev, Stalingrad, Leningrad, and other Soviet cities, supposedly leaving Moscow alone so the city could be destroyed by land forces. The Soviet Union responded by hitting Los Angeles, San Francisco, Las Vegas, Seattle, and Phoenix with their own nuclear weapons. The world war started when China launched hundreds of nuclear weapons onto both Japan and Taiwan, and then brutally invaded Hong Kong, taking England by surprise, who attempted to strike back. The Middle East erupted into violence when Jordan, Syria, and Saudi Arabia invaded Israel, Pakistan was invaded by India, and Iraq finished off its war with Iran by using every weapon known to mankind.

"I think we helped initiate the war," Hawking said, after reading the files.

"What gives you that idea, Doctor?" asked Erickson.

"We kept the shuttle *Challenger* from exploding, so the shuttle crew in turn placed the last satellite in orbit for the Star Wars Defense Initiative. Long story short, the Soviets challenged SDI, which ended with nuclear missiles hitting their cities. Their response was to nuke American cities. With the two superpowers fighting, other countries started fighting each other, which began World War Three. After the nuclear weapons were exhausted, the United States and the Soviet Union began using ground troops and conventional weapons. The last major battle for the two countries was on September 5, 1998, only because there was barely anyone in the military left to continue the war. The last American president was in the year 2000, and he was killed when a terrorist blew up the White House. Official United States government files end the same week, while the rest are all personal files begun around 2002."

"I suggest all of you stop what you're doing, put your hands up, and turn around, very slowly." A voice said from behind the time travelers.

As everyone did as they were told, the man who told them to turn around was holding an old Winchester rifle, along with ten other men who were also bristling with much heavier weapons. What was odd to the time travelers though, was that this man was the Vice President in the original timeline. He and his men walked into the room, confiscated Major Johnson and his teams' weapons and gear, and then ordered to nobody in particular, "Explain yourselves,"

"We are on a research mission from Alpha Centauri. Our ancestors left Earth during the war and we were sent to investigate what remained of Earth," Hawking stated hastily.

"Oh come on, you expect me to believe that story? I've been browsing through Pentagon, CIA, FBI, NSA, and other government files for years, and I see I have found the people responsible for this entire mess. That ship outside is the *USS Albert Einstein* and one of you is Doctor John Hawking. Now, explain to me what you're doing here,"

"This is the time we are from, so we were searching for answers on why we came back to a nuclear wasteland. I have a question for you though - how did anyone manage to stay in some semblance of the computer age in this ravaged land?"

"It hasn't been an easy task. Around 2003, everyone on the East Coast of the United States decided to pool whatever resources they had left to try to stay as advanced as possible. Currently, we've managed to rebuild in some places to mid-twentieth century levels. My question is, if you're from this time period and that really is a time traveling ship outside, then where did you get that level of technology?"

"When we left, World War Three never happened. The Soviet Union fell completely apart in 1992 and the United States became the lone superpower. All we wanted to do was fix little things in history."

"If the East Coast is active, what happened to everyone else in the States?" asked Williamson.

"I don't know what you saw as you re-entered Earth, most of the cities on our planet were destroyed and billions of people killed. Los Angeles, for example, was first nuked by the Soviets, and then set on fire by Chinese and Soviet forces as they went through what was left. The fire burned for six months until a massive thunderstorm quenched the fire. Over four thousand miles square were blackened. From what I've been told by people who live in the western United States, Los Angeles is a nuclear wasteland, from Long Beach to Palm Springs to San Diego. Nobody has gone into the area for more than one hundred years since radiation is really high,"

"Would you happen to know how many people are alive on this continent?" asked Erickson.

"That's a complicated answer. We have normal humans and mutants,"

"Does it really matter all that much?" asked Williamson.

"Unfortunately, it does. Around 2000, China made a last-ditch effort by dusting the jet stream with bio-chemicals to try to kill off the rest of the American population. What actually happened was that when the chemicals combined with nuclear poisoning in some people, those people became mutated along with their offspring. Now, one hundred and fifty years later, we have people who watch those mutant tribes for normal humans being born, and then we set up defense perimeters so the mutants can't raid our towns,"

"Why watch for normal humans being born amongst mutants?" asked Hawking.

"After the first couple of decades with these conditions, my predecessors noticed normal humans among the mutants. The normals acted a bit like the humans in that old ape movie, except the normals were all leaders of their various tribes. They led successful food raids on surviving towns, so it was decided that it needed to be stopped. So we watch for normals being born, and when given the chance, we extract the babies or toddlers so they can lead respectively normal lives,"

"How many normals have your people extracted?" asked Commander Smith.

"In the last one hundred years, I'd say we've extracted about two hundred and fifty normals. Unfortunately, every year more and more are being born, making our task much harder," responded the vice president.

"So, altogether, how many people are left in the United States?" asked Williamson.

"There are about thirty million scattered between both oceans and our northern and southern borders. So, what do you plan on doing since Earth is completely different from the way you left it?"

"I'd say it's simple, relatively speaking, of course. We travel back to the Jimmy Carter and Ronald Reagan administrations to ask them to stop what they're doing, and then we present them the choices they went with originally," answered Hawking.

"How do you know you'll not come back to this? As far as you know, this is the way the future is once you've changed it, or this is some type of alternate timeline-different dimension-parallel universe type of thing," remarked the Vice President.

"We know this isn't a parallel or alternate anything because I was in a separate ship and already here when they returned from their mission. If this was a parallel or alternate universe, there should be versions of ourselves here, unless of course, we have the whole grandfather paradox going on here too. I suggest we go back to fix some things," responded Williamson.

"I think we should just stay here. I'm getting sick and tired of going back and forth through time, especially if we go back to just change things none of you like. We have the technology, we can help rebuild civilization." remarked an irritated Commander Smith.

"Commander, we might be able to rebuild civilization, but I have a family and they may not exist here. I'd rather fix the past and come back to a timeline where my family is intact. You can stay here while the rest of us leave." ordered Williamson.

"I have a thought - Smith, you can watch what happens on a planetary scale when time changes, since we already know what happens in space?" Hawking asked.

"Fine, whatever."

Fifteen minutes later, the *Einstein* flew off, while Smith, the Vice President, and his people began walking towards Pennsylvania Avenue. Smith figured that if time did change, they would need to be near the White House, because the Pentagon could be a dangerous place to be if you weren't authorized to be there. The Vice President was telling Smith various stories about what had happened to Washington, when suddenly, the sun began to move back to the east. For a few minutes, the sky was dark, but the sun began rising again. As daylight washed over the city again for the second time in a day, Commander Smith saw what looked like a shockwave coming through the city. Inside of the shockwave, everything appeared distorted, as if everything was phasing in and out of the space-time continuum.

"Commander, what do we do?"

"Your guess would be as good as mine. I suppose we just let it overtake us. What harm could it do?"

As the shockwave overtook the men, everything appeared warped to Smith. He began to feel dizzy and sick to his stomach. He looked over at the vice president, who was distorted too, and phasing in and out of existence, or so it seemed to Smith. The Commander began getting sensory overload, when suddenly, a colorful explosion made him pass out.

Chapter 10

The *USS Albert Einstein* re-appeared in 2156, and almost immediately, Williamson ordered Yeager to contact the *Freedom Space Station*. Minutes went by before Yeager said, "I have a confirmed radio signal from all stations, but I don't get an answer. I conducted a sensor sweep for life signs and all personnel are accounted for. It appears to me as though everyone is asleep,"

"Can you tell or even confirm that our timeline is back to normal?" asked Captain Erickson.

"I couldn't tell you from here, Captain."

"Well, set course for Washington and land us at Lafayette Park."

Before the *Einstein* entered the atmosphere, both the *Freedom* and the *Luna Shipyards* appeared to be as normal as they were previously. The ship set down in the park, the crew left the timeship, and went across the street to the White House. Lieutenant Robinson found Commander Smith and Vice President Anderson lying on the ground, apparently unconscious. Robinson called the other time travelers over, and said, "Looks like the Vice President is wearing what he had been wearing before we left the first time."

"Can either of them be awakened?" asked a concerned Williamson.

Before anyone attempted to find out, Smith woke up, sat up, looked around, and asked, "Is everything back to normal?"

"As far as we know, Commander, but looks can be deceiving." replied Erickson.

"We need to investigate just how normal everything really is when we get back into the White House. Do you remember anything, Commander, about what happened after we left?" asked Hawking.

"The Vice President and I were nearing the burned out remains of the White House, when the sun reversed direction and re-set in the east. For a minute or so the sky was dark, but the sun began to rise again. With the rising sun, it brought with it a weird looking shockwave. The shockwave made everything appear distorted, making everything appear to phase in and out of existence. It descended onto Anderson and I, making me feel dizzy and sick, as if I was suffering from vertigo. I saw Anderson phasing in and out, but then I suffered from what I think was sensory overload. I can't say for certain what the shockwave was doing, but I do know I never want to experience that again."

Vice President Anderson woke up, looked around, and demanded, "What am I doing out here? What on Earth is going on?"

"What is the last thing you remember?" asked Hawking.

"I was working in my office when a staff member rushed in and told me something strange was approaching the city. I was preparing to leave when whatever it was came over me and made me feel horribly sick. Everything around me looked distorted, and I think all of my senses were overwhelmed. I must've passed out, because the next thing I know, I'm out here talking to you,"

"Do either of you feel sick or abnormal now?"

"No, I just don't like the effects of when time literally changes around me. I hope everything is fixed." responded Smith.

"I'd like to know what's going on," demanded Anderson.

"When we returned to 2156, we found an Earth devastated by nuclear war. We found out that we helped along events which had never originally occurred, like the Star Wars Defense Initiative for example, which was activated instead of a treaty being signed with the Soviet Union. When we landed in the war-ravaged version of 2156, we went to the Pentagon, accessed a computer, found out what happened, and then left to repair what went wrong," briefed Hawking.

"Did I happen to be in this alternate timeline?"

"It wasn't exactly an alternate timeline, but, yes you were. You were the leader of what was left of the northeastern United States, and you a few others tried to keep those left from slipping back into the Dark Ages,"

"How did you manage to stop a nuclear war?" asked the Vice President.

"We went to the late 1970's to talk to President Carter. One of the reasons the Star Wars program was started was become someone convinced Carter that the Earth could be threatened by an alien invasion force. We had to call in former President Kennedy to convince Carter otherwise. After Carter was assured nothing like an alien invasion was occurring, he signed the treaty with the Soviet Union,"

"President Kennedy was still alive? I thought he was assassinated in 1963?" asked Anderson.

"You still remember Kennedy being assassinated?" asked Erickson.

"Yes, don't you?"

"We all do, but we assumed you or anyone else wouldn't since you've never left 2156. I'll have to do some investigation into that phenomenon. To tell the story, one of our missions was to prevent his assassination, we succeeded. Kennedy informed us that Vice President Johnson, J. Edgar Hoover, the New York Mob, and Cuban terrorists were trying to kill him. Kennedy gave the CIA permission to take out Fidel Castro by any means necessary, so they killed him and the top Cuba leadership. Cuba itself was turned back into a territory of the United States, and eventually was given statehood," said Hawking.

"I remember Castro controlling Cuba until 2009, and his brother controlling Cuba for another fifteen years. This is too weird,"

Yes, we feel the same way. Then we visited President Reagan to ask him not to pursue the ballistic missile program, we even told him of what the consequences would be if he did. He had been briefed about all of our visits and he even remembered when Carl Sagan was at Edwards Air Force Base telling him and John Glenn about a starship in orbit around Venus. Reagan told us that President Nixon had read about all the other visits by the *USS Einstein,* becoming paranoid enough to come up with the Star Wars program, but he resigned from office, since Watergate still happened, before he had the chance to initiate the program. However, he managed to convince Carter to start up the program, until we showed up and set Carter on the right path. Reagan decided not to continue the ballistic missile program, and announced the creation of the B-1 and B-2 stealth bombers, which is what originally happened," answered Hawking.

"I knew you went back in time to retrieve Colonel Drayka and his JTFS people, but what do they have to do with all of this?" asked the Vice President.

"We aren't exactly sure what Colonel Drayka was really doing, but I think the rogue FBI agents used him to start this whole mess with Roswell. We found out that Drayka disappeared sometime after the *Einstein* left 1947, and his cohorts were sent to Alcatraz, where they all eventually died. In a few days, I'll order a strike on the JTFS headquarters." remarked Williamson.

"Do you know if history has returned to a relatively normal state?" asked Anderson.

"I won't know until I access a computer," responded Hawking.

The group had walked into the White House while they were talking and ended up at a computer in one of the offices. Doctor Hawking accessed the computer and began a search. After twenty minutes, the Doctor said, "A few things have changed. Before we went back in time, Texas, for example, had been divided into the Republic of Texas and the state of Texas because of the last Civil War. Due to our interference, the second Civil War never occurred, and Texas remains intact as a state in the Union. Unfortunately, something else happened.

"In the original timeline, the Y2K computer bug never happened, but this time it caused major disruptions. President Gary Jackson declared martial law after everything shut down, suspended the Constitution, ordered Congress to go on a lengthy recess, and then he declared himself Supreme Leader. Since communications were spotty at best, most Americans had no clue about what was going on, and according to this, if people did know, they didn't care unless a dictatorship hurt their pocketbook.

"The Presidential Elections were supposed to be later that year, but due to Jackson taking over, he had the Republican challenger, Senator Jason Lane of Utah, executed on the grounds of treason. The United States military, after he had tried to disband them and absorb them into a Civilian Defense Force, decided to work against Jackson subversively, since he allied the United States with other dictatorships around the world, including Iran and China. Jackson gave orders to shoot protestors dead on the spot, which began turning the American people against him.

"When communications were finally restored a year later and Americans found out what was happening, especially in the South and Rocky Mountain regions, a rebellion began. Those in the former military not loyal to the dictator, teamed up with rebels, and began a guerilla war against Chinese forces who had come to the United States to assist in keeping Jackson in power. This went on for eight months, until Jackson was on board *Air Force One*, which was guarded by Chinese MiG's, and a squadron of F-15's attacked the Chinese aircraft, destroying the MiG's quite readily. The F-15's had to shoot down the Presidents' plane because all warnings to land were ignored. Hours later, his wife and daughter, Mikayla and Tasha Jackson, along with Vice President Greg Phillips and his family, were rounded up, and then executed as traitors to the United States.

"The dictatorship lasted for five years, resulting in changes for the government. Some of which was that presidential candidates were required to submit to background checks, and had a psychological profile made of them. Congress took back the power that the President and other administrations had taken from them, and those powers not specifically granted to the federal government were given back to the states. So, now we have a more decentralized federal government.

"With Jackson gone, China tried to invade the United States, seeing the country as weak and easy to take without any leadership. Unfortunately for them, the United States military was prepared and stopped any major battles before they began. After kicking out the remaining Chinese soldiers on American territory, the United States military decided not to invade the Chinese mainland since too many people would get killed and the region could destabilize. You know, I'm beginning to regret inventing time travel after reading this, since it seems like everything is turning out wrong." remarked Hawking.

"Doctor Hawking, we've done a lot of good, like fixing the *Apollo 13*, the shuttle *Challenger*, and saving more passengers off the *Titanic*. Just because a few things didn't come off as planned, doesn't mean you should do something drastic, like destroying the *Einstein*. Thanks to you, I've learned a lot from time traveling." remarked Erickson.

"I've learned a lot too, Doctor. As an engineer, I thought twentieth century engineers had sort of an easy time of it, until I had to work on the *Apollo 13* and the *Challenger*. Those ships had very complex systems and I can see why everyone had such problems repairing them. I thank you for the history lesson." stated Robinson.

"Don't thank me too much. I also read that the *Apollo 13*, when about to take off from the moon, had a systems failure in the rockets and failed to achieve lift-off. NASA came up with a plan and had the *Apollo 14* on the launch pad two days later to rescue Lovell and Haise. Thirty seconds after lift-off, the *Apollo 14* exploded, and the *Apollo 13* astronauts died days later when the carbon dioxide scrubbers quit working and the two men died of asphyxiation. NASA left the spacecraft on the moon, and when they finally managed to establish a base, turned the area surrounding it into a museum, and never opened or touched the *Apollo 13* since it was considered a gravesite. Now, the *Challenger* shuttle made it all the way to 1996, but then it disintegrated in re-entry over Texas due to structural failure to a cracked wing, which was caused by foam falling off the rocket booster and hitting the wing on take-off. It seems the *Challenger* and *Apollo 13* were doomed from the start, and that shuttle replaced the *Columbia* as the ship that broke apart. I'm sure if I look hard enough, every mission we were involved in still had something that happened for the worse instead of the better," Hawking sighed.

"Maybe you could fix the Y2K bug so the dictatorship wouldn't happen," offered Williamson.

"That computer bug was so widespread that I wouldn't know where to begin. As for the dictatorship, it may happen no matter what we do, and fixing a computer programming error could just delay the inevitable,"

"You know, I may not like time travel, but I have learned one thing," Smith began to say, with some sarcasm in his voice.

"What would that be, Commander?" asked Williamson.

"Humans always have been and always will be nothing but idiots."

"Commander isn't that more than a bit harsh?" asked Erickson.

"Just chalk it up to another one of his negative opinions. If you feel that way, Mr. Smith, then I'll just have you re-assigned to a deep space mission far from here once all ships have been equipped with the new matter-antimatter stardrives." answered Williamson.

"Anyway, since I don't see any use for the *Einstein* or the *Time Tripper* any longer, why do we keep them?" asked an increasingly depressed Hawking.

"Now, hold on there, Doctor Hawking. We can use the ships for limited tourism to the past, teaching schoolchildren about history while it's happening, and the historians can actually see what happens. Of course, Congress would have to approve the whole idea," remarked Williamson.

Suddenly, one of the White House staff members burst in, looking for the president, and said," Mr. President, we just received a call from the Mayor of New York City,"

"Did she say what it was about?"

"Yes, she did. This may sound unbelievable, because it sure seems that way to me, sir. She said that the World Trade Center is still standing as if they had never been destroyed!"

"I think I can believe it, let me find out why." Hawking returned to the computer. Minutes later, he said, "According to this, several factors led to four airplanes from being hijacked. One was the fact that Israeli Prime Minister Rabin, who had been assassinated originally, kept Yasser Arafat in check and prevented him from gaining a huge following of Islamic extremists. In turn, this made the Taliban and Osama bin Laden in Afghanistan very isolated and not a single country aided his cause, including other Middle East countries. The hijackers, who tried to take control of two United and two American Airlines, were stopped at Logan Airport in Boston, and were arrested before they could do any significant damage. This had occurred in 2001 in our original timeline, but these events happened in 2006. Do we have a live web camera focused on the World Trade Center?"

The staffer went over to the computer, typed in an address, and the screen popped up with a clear picture of the New York City skyline. The camera focused on the Trade Centers as they basked in the glow of the mid-day sun. Everyone was shocked, so Williamson asked, "Did the mayor say anything else?"

"No, sir. She's waiting for word from you on what she should do next."

"I suppose it's time to give New York yet another visit then."

A day later, a huge amount of government officials, both federal and state, made their way into what was supposed to be two completely different buildings, designed to honor the fallen World Trade Center and the people who died there, but instead they entered two buildings that had been built in 1973, which were supposed to have been destroyed in 2001.

Amazingly enough, business that were scattered around the city of New York, were now inside the buildings as if nothing had ever happened. President Williamson held a press conference to make known the events of the *Einstein's* missions, which prompted the American public into finding out more. After the New York visit, the president ordered a strike on the JTFS headquarters, with Japan's permission, only to find empty buildings. No paperwork, no people, no computers, absolutely nothing. Williamson ordered that it be destroyed anyway.

The crew of the *Einstein* all became famous. Hawking ended up with many requests for him to appear on talk shows, requests from historians to take them on time travel trips, and even requests from school districts asking if they could go back in time on field trips for their children. For Hawking, it got the point where he had to hire a secretary to keep track of his schedule and an agent who could keep people from demanding so much from the scientist. Even though he was still relatively young, there were times he felt much older since he was being pulled in one direction or another, and sometimes regretted inventing the means to travel through time, even though it made him rich beyond his wildest dreams. For a time, the scientist was bugged by the fact that he could never figure out who had tried to stop him on those first missions back in time, even though he did try for a while to investigate whatever leads there were, but those leads always hit a dead end.

Erickson continued to captain the *Einstein* for ten more years, eventually taking archeologists, school children, historians, and some tourists back in time to witness events in history.

Yeager also stayed with the ship, and managed to witness his ancestor Chuck Yeager break the sound barrier. Lieutenant Robinson was promoted to captain's rank, and continued to be an engineer, constantly trying to refine the matter-antimatter stardrives so that starships could go even faster, and he also developed a way for time travelers not to pass out when they go back and forth through time.

Commander Smith was sent on a deep space mission by President Williamson and the Pentagon, but resigned a year later to begin his crusade to stop time travel. In spite of the United States government trying to make him look like a lunatic, he developed a following, including his own son. In the early 2200's, Smith's son decided to become the leader of rogue time travelers, to try to stop Hawking and the crew of the *Einstein* from changing the course of human history.

When a timeship ended up stolen fifty years later, Hawking doesn't realize it was that same timeship they had destroyed in the 1940's. The United States government, after always having a problem with security involving the small fleet of time traveling ships, decides to abandon time travel altogether after the *Max Planck* is stolen by those rogue time travelers. Of course, this doesn't stop time travel completely, because Hawking disappears shortly after the government announces their intentions. Nobody knew if Hawking went back in time, or if he just went into hiding, but since time traveling is now officially banned, no one will know for sure.

~The End~

*****

Don't miss out!

Visit the website below and you can sign up to receive emails whenever Cliff Ball publishes a new book. There's no charge and no obligation.

https://books2read.com/r/B-A-IE-HJ

BOOKS 2 READ

Connecting independent readers to independent writers.

Did you love *Out of Time: a Time Travel Novel*? Then you should read *New Frontier: An Alternate History Novel*[1] by Cliff Ball!

[2]

In this alternate history novel, what-if Ronald Reagan became President in 1976 instead? The President continues with the moon landings and declares that a moon base would be established by 1979, followed by a Mars Base by 1989. In the meantime, the Soviets decide to up the ante. We follow America's progress from the moon to Mars, along with the Teacher in Space Program, to an eventual starship mission out of the solar system, which will continue in book two, Final Frontier.

Read more at cliffball.net.

---

1. https://books2read.com/u/boo7ab

2. https://books2read.com/u/boo7ab

Also by Cliff Ball

An American Journey
The Long Journey - Christian Historical Fiction

New Frontier
New Frontier: An Alternate History Novel
Final Frontier: A Time Travel Novel

Perilous Times
The Falling Away - Christian End Times Novel
The Great Deception
The Great Tribulation
The Perilous Times Box Set - A Christian End Times Series

The End Times Saga
Times of Turmoil: A Christian Thriller
Times of Trouble: Christian End Times Novel
Times of Trial: Christian End Times Thriller
Times of Rebellion: A Christian Novel

Times of Destruction: A Christian End Times Thriller
Times of Judgment: A Christian End Times Thriller
Times of Tribulation: Christian End Times Thriller
Times of Harvest: A Short Story Collection
The End Times Saga Box Set: A Christian Fiction Series

Standalone
Out of Time: a Time Travel Novel
Dust Storm: Christian Western Short Story
The Usurper: A Christian Political Thriller
Don't Mess With Earth: An Alternate History Novel

Watch for more at cliffball.net.

About the Author

Cliff Ball lives in Texas, born in Arizona, and is a Christian. Has two BA's and a Certificate in Technical Communications. Has published sixteen novels and four short stories. Won third in high school for a short story written in Creative Writing class for a young adult magazine. Visit his website to find out more about him and his novels: cliffball.net

Read more at cliffball.net.